BLURRING
THE LINES

MEN OF THE ZODIAC

MARISA CLEVELAND

Entangled Publishing, LLC
2614 South Timberline Road
Suite 109
Fort Collins, CO 80525
Visit our website at www.entangledpublishing.com.

Indulgence is an imprint of Entangled Publishing, LLC.

Edited by Robin Haseltine
Cover design by Heather Howland
Cover art from Shutterstock

Manufactured in the United States of America

First Edition November 2015

For my husband.
All the best moments in my life happen because of him.

Aquarius:
Intellectual, sexual, selfless humanitarian with a distant,
rebellious side.

Chapter One

B lake Whitman approached The Fresh Bean, the oldest coffeehouse in Edgewater Bay, and inhaled. If any morning called for coffee, it was today.

"I'm so sorry!"

He heard the apology a split second before a tiny terrier buzzed by him, cutting to the right and forcing him to stop his momentum.

What the— Unfortunately, another dog followed the first, and when Blake stepped to the side, his ankle caught on the leash. His foot locking in place, his upper body crashed into something soft—a girl? He gripped her bare shoulders, and as his hands tightened on her impossibly smooth skin, he angled his body so when they tumbled to the pavement in a tangle of limbs and fur, it was his back that took the fall.

They landed nose to nose. Amid the earthy smell and the unmistakable pet scent, he inhaled *her*, all warm and fresh and womanly, making him forget the pain shooting down his spine. All his carefully crafted Monday morning plans disappeared under the weight of the woman blinking her dark eyes and regarding him with a mixture of laughter and concern.

Something sharp — a knee — landed in his thigh.

"Oh!" Her gasp came right before an open palm pressed his face, the side of his head, his chest, as she twisted out of his arms. "Are you okay?"

She scooted back and patted his stomach, his hip — But all movement froze when her hand brushed over the zipper on his pants. With her ponytail swinging to the side, she looked down to that area and grinned, her chest rising and falling with rapid succession.

Without waiting for his answer, the woman scrambled to her feet. He'd barely had time to register her shy smile or the tempting press of her limbs. She crouched and grabbed her fallen papers, shuffling them into a disorderly stack. When he tried to sit up, a large and very shaggy dog climbed over his face, perching both paws on his stomach, tail slapping across his face. Two more culprits jumped and barked by his ear. If he moved, the dogs might bolt, and he'd hate to have to help her chase down three escaped mutts this early in the morning. He wasn't sure he could, anyway, until his back stopped aching.

Pinned in place, he watched her brush down her sundress and mutter as she retrieved the leashes. Finally, mercifully, she noticed him still on the ground, immobilized by a Bearded Collie, a Scottish Terrier, and the chocolate Labrador.

"Muffin, no!" The brunette, stuffing the pile of papers under one arm and unwrapping the knotted leashes with the other, tugged the Scottish Terrier back, only to let the first two dogs descend on him and lick him like his face was bacon. "Oh!"

Her gaze landed on his, and Blake swore through the initial shock he saw a glint of mirth. Glad *she* found his predicament funny… "Uh — ?"

"Don't worry, dude. Their tongues haven't been anywhere suspicious in the last hour."

Had she really just called him dude? He was thirty, not thirteen, and this was southwest Florida, not California. All concern for his person disappeared from her expression, her smile betraying her amusement. She was pretty in a fresh-faced, passion-for-life way, and he let the nickname slide.

Once she managed to pull the two largest beasts from his body, he plucked up the first offender and stood. The terrier continued to stretch its tongue toward his mouth, even after he placed the dog back on the cement.

She grinned up at him. "I tried to warn you."

That split-second apology had been her warning?

They faced each other, and he found it adorable how she struggled to maintain her balance as the dogs tugged and moved in different directions. Blake had never been so instantly aware of someone. She must have felt it, too, because he saw the slightest hint of shock in her dark eyes.

He conceded, "I guess you did."

She opened her mouth at the same time Haley, the coffeehouse manager, flew from the shop. "Mr. Whitman! Are you okay? I saw the whole thing."

"Morning, Haley. We seem to be fine, I think." He glanced at the woman still struggling to put order to the three dogs and pile of papers. "Do you need help?"

"Kira, my God, you could have killed Mr. Whitman!" Haley made a tsking noise and then held out a paper cup to him. "Here. I brought you your usual triple espresso."

The brunette frowned. "All that caffeine isn't healthy."

Had she just chided him...a stranger? For drinking coffee? Her audacity intrigued him. Although he was tempted to debate the merits of caffeine with her, he didn't have time to spare, even for a little innocent flirtation. His real estate investment firm wouldn't run itself, and he was already late.

"Kira!" Haley's shocked gasp clicked him back to reality.

The brunette's mouth opened into an "O" and then

snapped shut. She glanced at him from beneath her bangs and gave him a small grin. "I didn't mean it like it sounded."

Damn, she had a sexy mouth. He didn't take his gaze off her lips as he said, "I'm sure you didn't." He took the cup from Haley. "Thank you."

Haley beamed. "Anything for you, Mr. Whitman." She turned to Kira. "Mr. Whitman donated five Peter Maxx paintings to the animal rescue's silent auction last spring."

"Oh. What a generous donation."

He cringed, ready for the usual stream of compliments about his generosity. When it didn't come, and she merely gave him a friendly, easygoing smile, he grinned back. He liked that she didn't go on and on about it, even though she seemed to be a real animal lover. That kind of thing embarrassed the hell of out of him.

Haley laughed. "No. I don't think you get it. This is *the* Blake Whitman."

"It's such a pleasure to meet you, *the* Blake Whitman." The brunette stuck out her hand, the one that wasn't holding the leashes, but with the flyers tucked under her arm precariously, she quickly retracted it. "I'm even sorrier I didn't stop Muffin from tripping you."

Her words sounded sincere, but amusement still flickered in her eyes. Her seeming lack of interest fascinated him. If he didn't have a major development proposal to tackle that would change the face of the downtown Edgewater Bay area, he'd probably stick around to question whether apologizing for her dogs was genuine.

"The pleasure is mine, Kira." He said her name and liked the way it sounded. He removed the cup's lid and gulped back the espresso.

"Did the brew come out okay?" Haley chewed on her lower lip.

"It's perfect," he said to her, but he couldn't drag his

attention from Kira. He kept his focus on her as he reached into his pocket, retrieved a ten, and handed it to Haley. "Thanks for personally delivering it."

She slipped the bill into her apron and winked. "Anything for you."

A group of teens entered The Fresh Bean, and Haley gave an apologetic wave. "Better get in there. Looks like the morning rush is starting."

Kira faced Blake. "I really am sorry about Muffin. I hope you're okay and not just saying that to be polite."

Okay, maybe he'd read her wrong. That had sounded earnest enough. He bent down to scrub a hand over Muffin's tiny head. When the dog jumped to attention, he scooped her up with one arm and scratched her behind the ear. "This little lady? I'm glad I didn't land on her."

Kira coughed. "Him." A smile twitched at the corners of her full lips.

"You named a boy dog Muffin?"

"You sound surprised."

He stroked the top of Muffin's head. "Poor fellow."

She handed him one of the flyers pressed to her chest. "And if you have an issue with that, we're having an adopt-a-thon this weekend. Feel free to adopt him and change his name to whatever suits you."

He took the flyer with the Edgewater Animal Rescue logo. Should he tell her he'd donated more than the Peter Maxx paintings to the organization? He'd also been one of ten donors—he'd donated anonymously—to fund the first dog park at the beach.

Ridiculous. Since when had he needed a female's stamp of approval for his actions? "Okay, well, thanks for the info."

Apparently bored with the human interaction, the dogs had fallen silent and lounged on the pavement. Kira wiggled their leashes. "I better get these guys their breakfast."

Blake lifted his empty cup in farewell. "Take care."

He was a little sad to see her go. She was the most interesting woman he'd met in a while. She probably wasn't available anyway because she had a boyfriend or husband. But he hadn't seen a ring, and she'd stiffened when she'd heard his last name. Then again, maybe he'd imagined the whole attraction thing.

So why was he regretting not asking for her number?

Blake Whitman. So that was the guy. The CEO of the company her father mentioned had wanted to buy the building. She looked at The Fresh Bean storefront and the floors above it.

What would happen to the not-for-profits using the second floor as their headquarters and the pro bono lawyers working out of the community room for special projects? Where would they go? What about Haley? Would she, and all the coffeehouse staff, lose their jobs?

The brick building had been a gift from her dad to her mom, which had reverted back to her father after her mom had died. If he sold it now, her mom's vision would never come true. Everything her mom had sacrificed would be for nothing.

According to her dad, the Whitman-Madison team led the drive for redevelopment into a shiny new downtown for Edgewater Bay, but their vision clashed with her mom's idea for preserving this tract as the historic section of town. With a population topping twenty thousand, the city had experienced growth over the past two decades, and with more and more tourists flocking to the sandy beaches, everyone agreed there was a need to revitalize the area—but not everyone agreed which direction to take. A quaint, but rambling, main street had developed along the bay, and last month the city council voted on a firm—Whitman-Madison—to redefine the area. She'd read articles and heard rumors of franchises replacing local, family-owned shops, and had wondered how to stop it from happening.

Kira's chest squeezed, and her anger at Blake's company for wanting to tear down the beautiful brick building resurfaced.

It would be a shame to give up such a large piece of her mom's legacy to a real estate development company. The Whitman-Madison reputation for dollars before heart filled the front page of the business section more often than not. She didn't understand how the firm—a family-founded company—could put aside small town values in favor of corporate greed.

Kira led the dogs around back to where a makeshift gated area had been designed for them. After she opened the fence, they ran down the strip of grass to the end and back again. She hadn't been kidding about getting them breakfast, and as was her morning tradition, she spoiled whichever dogs from the rescue she happened to be walking that day to gourmet, dog-friendly treats from The Fresh Bean.

Muffin licked her ankle and she picked up the terrier, cuddling him to her. She squinted up at the back of the building.

After filling the dogs' bowls with fresh water, she stepped through the back door and made her way through the oldest coffeehouse in town. The interior lacked the modern feel of other franchised cafes, but she found it comforting that not everything old had to be replaced. Sure, the wood floors had seen better days, but the building had been her mother's brainchild to create a central location for philanthropic endeavors, and while other shops had come and gone, The Fresh Bean had continued to thrive and lease the first floor, providing enough income to cover the basic utilities for the other floors to operate.

She had to do something.

Her roommate worked for Whitman-Madison. Perhaps she could meet with this guy. Tell him about the hard work, planning, and dedication that went into forming The Bromwell. The value of the location for the non-profits. Maybe he'd hear her out. More likely he'd be too busy.

Seeing Blake up close, and not just from newspaper pictures of society functions with some woman on his arm, reminded her of all the reasons she'd left her first job. He seemed in a rush to get to the coffee shop, gulped his drink then dashed off, probably to hurry to the office and sift through mountains of paperwork.

Yet even with his harried demeanor, Blake looked hot in his suit—like the pressure-filled job fit him. And he'd smiled—several times—at her and picked up Muffin, despite all the fur the dog left on his jacket, so he might not be so cold-hearted after all. Unless she read him wrong, he'd been interested in her. Not enough to ask for her number, but he might listen to a concerned resident about saving the building.

After all, she was a smart, independent woman. Why couldn't she tempt him into changing his mind—and maybe getting him to ask for her number?

Chapter Two

B lake arrived at the office with the intriguing Kira still on his mind.

His secretary Margie stood as he approached her desk. She fidgeted with the notepad in her hand and then handed him several phone messages that he scanned.

"Please put these on my calendar to call back this afternoon. I'm determined to get through at least a quarter of this contract"—he held up his briefcase—"before my eight thirty."

"This came by certified mail."

He tore open the package she indicated and pulled out a rather thick contract. After reading the cover and introduction, he swore and looked at the date and time stamp. Twenty minutes ago. When he'd been wrangling rescue mutts instead of reviewing properties.

"Sorry. This means another late night."

She rolled her eyes. "What's new?"

Blake thought he heard her mutter something under her breath, but he ignored it and gave her a curt nod. "Excellent.

Tell Tyler I'll need him, too, please." It wouldn't hurt to have their CIO on hand to handle the technical terminology.

Margie gripped her coffee mug, reminding Blake of his morning encounter with Kira and her dogs. His secretary's lips moved slightly as she continued to stare blankly at him, and he thought he heard her counting to ten before she blinked and shot him her usual close-mouthed smile. "Whatever you say, boss."

Her tone caught his attention. "You won't be alone, Margie. I'll be here, too."

"You always are."

He had no response to his secretary's shockingly flippant answer, but he didn't dictate when the head of a major information systems manufacturing firm would spare time to listen to Whitman-Madison's most recent pitch for commercial expansion.

Masking his irritation, he said, "Thank you."

Margie nodded. "I'll let Tyler know. Also, I'll hold all calls and let you know when your eight thirty arrives."

"Excellent. Thank you." Blake entered his corner office, placed his briefcase on the floor, and sank into his chair. Then, he swiveled around and stared out the window. His office faced the south part of the bay. If he had his younger brother, Keith's, office, overlooking the city, he might be able to see The Fresh Bean building. He frowned. One more thing that needed his attention on his already overloaded plate. Kira's flyer crinkled in his pocket, and he tossed it into the wooden tray amid the stack of other important items.

Two pages into the second section of the contract from the city council, a commotion sounded outside his door, but he ignored it. If they needed him, Margie would know to interrupt. A couple more muffled sounds, a sharp clicking of heels on the hardwood floors, and then silence. It was too quiet. With a heavy sigh, he opened the door.

Darcy, his brother's secretary, stood with her hand raised to knock. "Blake, Keith would like to speak with you."

Regretting yet another disruption, he checked the clock then strode into Keith's office and shut the door.

Keith opened a drawer and removed a tie. "Your secretary quit. That's the tenth one this year."

Blake stared at his younger brother. He'd thought she was fine. Why did she go to Keith to quit and not tell him? He sighed. "So, Margie quit. Doesn't surprise me. I asked her to stay late tonight, and she seemed put out. She knows my schedule."

"This doesn't look good. We need to discuss our image."

"You're twenty-five, VP for a multi-million dollar real estate investment firm, and since you started three years ago, you've had the same secretary. *Your* image is fine."

Keith tossed a tabloid across the desk at Blake. *New Doesn't Always Mean Better.* The article expounded on the latest endeavor at Whitman-Madison, a shiny, new downtown for Edgewater Bay, and pulled no punches in calling CEO Blake a man concerned only with profit.

"It wasn't my image I was concerned about. Between the ten secretaries who've quit, the several others you've fired, and the reference to us endorsing a throwaway society, we're developing a reputation for high turnover, like profit is our driving motive."

"We have a sterling business reputation. And this deal that you're hounding me about"—he pointed to the tabloid— "will increase our annual profits by 19%. I think that'll give our investors something else to talk about."

"Agreed, but public image is important, so let's diffuse the"—Keith made air quotes with his hands, actual friggin' air quotes—"'concerned only with the bottom line' accusation."

That sounded like a compliment to him, but Blake knew to pick his arguments. "Fine," he said. "I'll be sure to make some additional charity appearances. I'll increase my donations for this quarter."

Damn it, how was it that his local barista knew about his Peter Maxx donations, while the tabloids chose to overlook that and play up his more aggressive professional side? All right, he'd up his next contribution to a Lichtenstein. His smile took on a hard edge. "I'll play nicer for the sake of the press."

"And for your next secretary? You know I don't involve myself in your office, but all joking aside, if we're not careful, your former employees will band together about workplace conditions, and we'll wind up with a class action suit on our hands."

Keith always had a flare for the dramatics.

"I adhere with all OSHA requirements."

A tiny vein pulsed in his brother's temple. Good, Blake shouldn't be the only one with high blood pressure this morning. "Over a dozen secretaries in two years would suggest otherwise."

Okay, so a number of his secretaries had left of their own accord, but Blake had been forced to fire several. He'd never risk everything he and his family had worked for by dipping his pen in the company ink. He hadn't encouraged their advances, and he sure as hell had never acted on them. The whole situation was just so…frustrating.

He wasn't so arrogant to think the women genuinely lusted after him. Most of his, um, more amorous hires had seen him for his checkbook, and not much more than that.

"It's not my fault they act inappropriately," he said. "Or that they aren't willing to invest the time required of the position."

"So hire women who don't want to sleep with you."

"It's not like it's a prerequisite. They're hired because they can do the job and then—stuff happens." He shrugged.

Keith raked a hand through his hair. "Let's talk about

Margie quitting today. *She* wasn't interested in you. She's married with four children. Care to explain why she called you a tyrant and that a robot had more sensitivity than you?"

"We pay excellent overtime, and Margie said she was willing to work additional hours when I hired her."

"Yes, but overtime for most people means a couple extra hours a week, maybe the occasional Saturday meeting. You had her banking more hours than most of the junior associates in our legal department. Please, just hire a secretary who doesn't want to sleep with you, who won't quit in a month, and who likes to work long hours like you. Okay? And no more tabloids." Keith picked up his phone and muttered more to himself than to Blake. "I've got to get a press release drafted about the new medical center we're building on Palm Street to try and deflect the negative press of this downtown venture."

Blake left Keith's office and returned to his own, sinking into his chair. It aggravated him that his younger brother doled out advice, even if he was right. Blake cursed. Wasn't he the boss? He picked up the phone to call their recruiter. Cliff answered in half a ring. Now that impressed Blake.

"I need you to send over a list of potential secretaries."

"Again?" Cliff didn't bother masking his surprise.

"Find me someone who understands that overtime means more than a couple of hours, and maybe not married with kids or at least someone who'll comprehend the level of commitment needed for this position. Someone loyal."

Cliff snorted. "Sounds like you should hire a dog."

Chapter Three

The elevator doors slid open, and Kira stepped inside, pressing the fourth floor button and ignoring all her insecurities. She could do this. She could confront Blake. Guys like him were workaholic men with tunnel vision, and she'd dated enough of them. If she appealed to his ego first, she could get him to listen.

She smoothed her skirt and took a deep breath. Blake might refuse to see her. No doubt he'd be in the middle of something important. But she had to remember that her own goal — saving her mom's legacy — was equally important. That conviction carried her off the elevator and into the open space, where she cut a direct path to her roommate's office.

"Tish. I'm here."

Her roommate looked up from a file and grinned. "You brought me coffee!"

Kira shook her head. "No. It's not for you. Do you think this is a bad idea?"

Her friend stood and smiled. "Absolutely not, especially since you come with gifts."

A hot coffee could hardly be considered a gift, but she'd grabbed it with the intention of giving her a reason to enter his office and place it on the desk. That act alone would buy her a couple of prolonged seconds to plead her case. "What if he's in the middle of a meeting?"

"He's not." Tish rolled her eyes. "Did you mean what you said on the phone? About wanting to do something more than nothing?"

"Yes."

"Well, here's your shot. You're here. Take it." She pointed to the corner office at the opposite side of the room. "He's in there, and his secretary just quit this morning, so no one's guarding the door."

Again? The running joke at the apartment was how many girls Blake overworked or fired for coming on to him, and Kira tensed even more; he'd probably be in a bad mood. She should come back another day. Maybe wait until he'd hired someone — who could stop her from getting an appointment. No. Tish was right. This was her chance.

With no one protecting the open door, she took her time walking toward him, studying his bent head and thinking how to best approach him.

His diplomas were perfectly aligned on the right wall, along with a myriad of other certificates and achievements. Lining the credenza under the wall display were matching framed photos of Blake at various events or with other noteworthy people in the community.

Good. He took pride in his image. That could work in her favor.

He must have sensed someone hovering, because his gaze snapped directly to hers. "Kira?" He stood and gestured to the seat across his desk.

Even from across the room, the piercing sharpness of his eyes caught her in ways she didn't comprehend. He might be gorgeous, but his was still the handsome public face of the company eager to destroy the old and build brand new. Before she lost her nerve, she held up the coffee cup. "I brought you this. It's decaf, since I know you're probably already wired."

His dark eyebrows arched. "You came here to bring me a coffee?"

"Actually no." She stepped into the office and approached his desk without taking the offered seat. While placing the cup by his right hand, she wondered why she hadn't decided on an opening line to this discussion. She'd had plenty of time to concoct a speech on her way here, and yet, standing in front of him now, watching him assess her, the right words escaped her. "What a great view."

After uncapping the cup, he sipped, closing his eyes and swallowing, a smile curving his lips. As his eyelids opened, his grin widened. "Whatever reason brought you here, thank you. No need to apologize again, but I appreciate the gesture." He took another sip.

She stared at the way his mouth covered the lip of the cup. A flowing sound of sexy baritone notes made it challenging to piece together what his words actually meant. Apologize? That's what he thought?

"Mr. Whitman, I'm not here to apologize. I'm here to discuss The Bromwell Building and your plans for the revitalized downtown area."

That caught him off guard, if she judged the look in his eyes correctly. "Oh?"

He gestured once more the chair, and she decided it would be impolite to not sit down. She waited for him to sit, and then she took a deep breath. "A true pillar of the community would be celebrating and preserving this section of town and especially the building, not tearing it down."

"I don't disagree."

"But you still want to tear it down?"

"That remains an open conversation between myself and the board."

If he seemed surprised that she wanted to discuss it with him now, he didn't show it. The guy must win big at poker, because she couldn't tell what he was thinking.

"I read an article stating your intentions to tear down all the old buildings in favor of creating a more citified downtown." No need to mention the phone call her father received. In fact, he'd probably take her more seriously if she didn't mention her father.

"That's one plan on the table. But not everything you read in the media is correct."

She knew that, but with the way he crossed his arms over his chest and regarded her with a grain of annoyance, his strong jaw firm, his aristocratic nose slightly raised, he reminded her of all the entitled jerks from her Northeast prep school. She tightened her mouth into a straight line.

"Mr. Whitman, the whole street should be preserved as a local historical landmark."

He crossed his arms over his chest. "You make a good argument."

"Thank you." She couldn't tell by his expression whether or not he understood the importance of this to her.

"Quite the dilemma. Refurbish the old or tear it down and build something new." He tapped his finger to his lips.

"I'm invested in keeping the old. My family owns The Bromwell Building. My mother had a vision for its use until she passed away." Which wouldn't happen if he had his way.

"I'm sorry to hear that, and I'd like to help you."

Instead of relief at his words, her shoulders tensed, but she didn't drop her stare. Saying he wanted to help and actually conceding were miles apart. She met his gaze evenly as she replied, "Thank you."

As if sensing her rising anger, he shot her a wicked grin,

one that gave her the sense her reaction amused him. "I said I wanted to help you."

Okay, maybe he wasn't a double jerk. Just a jerk. A handsome jerk with bedroom eyes and—

"Kira, are you attracted to me in a sexual manner?"

Her jaw hinged open with an audible click. "Most certainly not!" Not in any way that would make a difference in this conversation.

"Excellent. And would you work to save this building—if you could?"

"Of course. I hardly expect to rely on your good graces. I'll rally the community, sign petitions, engage the local council and women's groups." Maybe, since she intended to take this as far as she needed to, she'd enlist her dad's connections with the mayor. Blake couldn't tear down the building if her dad refused to sell, even if the rest of the street wanted to.

"So you'd invest your personal time during the workday and extra hours after to achieve your goal?"

She didn't bother to hide the sarcasm. "No. I just stormed into your office unannounced, with no standing appointment, to plead my argument, only to leave here and abandon my plight and my family's heritage."

He chuckled. "So I can surmise that you won't quit. That you'll work tirelessly to achieve your goal."

"I work tirelessly to achieve all of my goals." Unfortunately, it sometimes took a bit longer to figure out what those goals were, but she had no doubt about this. Something solid and lasting—a tribute to her mom. So while she'd been searching for a crusade to tackle since leaving her father's firm so soon after graduating—which accounted for her sporadic volunteer efforts and her inability to find enough time to help out with every organization she wanted to champion—this was one battle she was willing to see through to the end.

B lake couldn't take his gaze from Kira, and ever since she'd entered his office, he'd fixated on her thick brown ponytail and white button-down shirt under a gray suit that didn't quite fit her properly. He sucked back his surprise not just at seeing her again so soon, but also in the way his breathing seemed to increase and slow down at the same time. How the heck did she elicit such a reaction from him? He hadn't lost his breath over a woman in a decade. Perhaps longer.

And yet, here he was, staring at the animal-rescue-volunteer-dog-walker who'd reprimanded him for needing a triple shot of espresso. His whole brain lit with quips and comebacks and ways to lure her into his…life.

The last thing he'd expected was facing Kira in his office with her monologue about saving a building. But in the face of his brother's morning lecture, an idea formed.

"So how committed are you?"

"Very," she said, her brows drawing together. She was pretty, even when she frowned. This idea forming in his head had disaster written all over it, but he couldn't stop himself.

"How fast can you type?"

She stared at him as if he had three heads. "Fast."

"Hmmm."

He steepled his fingers and leaned back, pleased at the timing of it all. "Interesting. And you're serious about doing whatever it takes for your cause."

This warranted a suspicious look from her. "Yes. Within reason."

"I see."

She leaned forward, her hands gripping the edge of his desk. "Do you? Because this happens to be the one time and the one thing that I'm not willing to let go of. I want to save that building."

"Perfect." Her determination encouraged him.

"You think it's perfect that I'm not going to let this go?"

"I find myself in need of a secretary. I'd like to offer that position to you."

"I beg your pardon? I didn't come here to get a job. I came here to warn you. I'm taking this to the next city council meeting. That building should not be demolished. There are plenty of other options for redeveloping downtown."

"I don't disagree."

She continued ranting as if she hadn't heard him. "You know what you are? You're one of those guys who thinks that I need a job, and that will shut me up. Well, it won't. Even if I worked for you, and I'd never work for you, I'd still do everything in my power to make sure the building was safe. And while we're on the subject, I'd make you loosen your purse strings for other community projects, too."

Was she for real? A part of him wanted to stand up and ask her if she even recognized the privilege she had in being allowed into his office, but he wasn't that big of an ass. He'd always had a half-open door policy. Still, it was rare for unannounced visitors to find him with even five minutes to spare, let alone find themselves at a receiving end of a lucrative job offer. And the *never work for you* flashed a red challenge light he couldn't ignore. She thought she had him pegged. "Loosen my purse strings? Can't say that I've ever had a purse."

She rolled her eyes. "Whatever. You might think the Peter Maxx donation was magnanimous of you, but I know that, given your projected tax bracket, your chief legal counsel should have banked for a higher deduction."

Impressive. And she'd just confirmed his initial assessment that she was smart. How smart, he didn't care. It was a secretarial position. But she knew how to use her words, and that attracted him more and more. "Be my secretary, and I'll let you be part of the solution."

"No."

"Plus, if you agree to stay for one year, I'll give you twenty percent from my own personal charity allowance to donate how you feel best fits this community's needs. With the money I plan to allocate, I bet you could save a lot of puppies."

Her cheeks pinkened, and her head tilted slightly when she asked, "Why?"

This was a bad idea. A really bad idea. But he felt compelled. He needed someone passionate and dedicated. He'd just have to keep his physical interest in her at bay. He could do that.

He was very good at getting what he wanted, and he'd decided—sometime in the past twenty minutes—that he wanted Kira. As his secretary. "Because I don't have a secretary, and if I did, I'm fairly confident we wouldn't be having a discussion right now."

She glanced at him from beneath her bangs and gave a small smile. "But why would you ask me? Why offer me the job?"

Because you can't stand me. And you'd be loyal. She'd been taking care of those animals and helping out her mother's charities. She had an end game, stakes in it, and that meant she'd be willing to do the job.

A spontaneous, very un-Blake thing to do? No doubt. But like his other business decisions, he wouldn't change course or second-guess himself.

"It's a good position. Full-time with benefits. It's a steady salary. Like I said, I find myself in need of a secretary, so I'm willing to pay what you feel is fair for a one-year commitment of your time. And you get to take care of all of your pet projects using my money. It's a good proposition."

The side of her mouth twitched, but he couldn't be sure

if she was smiling or smirking. "I didn't come here for a job. I came here to discuss my family's building."

"And we're negotiating. Come work for me, and I'll direct the architect to draft an alternate design for the community redevelopment."

She tensed, and when she sucked on her lower lip, he wondered what she tasted like, and frowned. Where had that thought come from?

"It's that simple?" He heard the suspicion in her voice.

"We're crunched for time, but new plans can be drafted. I'm not saying it will be simple, but I'll support a change in vision."

Her frown deepened. "But nothing's guaranteed."

He had a quip, but this wasn't the time to use it. "Whitman-Madison's board needs to approve it, as well as the community redevelopment board, but I think I have enough sway to make this happen." When she continued to eyeball him with doubt, he took a sip of the cooling coffee and reminded her, "Don't forget the charity allowance."

She clasped her hands in front of her. "The thing is, Haley, from The Fresh Bean, has been trying to get a job with you forever. And my roommate works in your accounting department."

"Your point?" *Interesting*. Her roommate already worked for him. He made a mental note to pull that file from HR.

The bewildered expression didn't leave her face. "You don't know anything about me."

Why was he having to convince her to work for him? Why wasn't she thanking him and hugging him for his generosity and leaping up and down for joy and asking when she should start? And why did her reluctance please him more than if she'd taken the job from the jump?

The confusion on her face fascinated him. It was like she couldn't quite figure out how to piece him together, but that she wasn't willing to quit just yet. "Look, Kira, I know enough. I know you're neat, organized, and smart. Smart enough to come down here with a list of reasons why the building should be saved."

"And that's enough? To offer me a job on the spot?"

This woman stopped him mid-thought. With every protest and argument out of her mouth, he solidified his desire to hire her as his secretary. She'd be dedicated and loyal, and no question she'd get the job done. She was the perfect solution to cleaning up his image.

With a carefree shrug he'd perfected over the years, he said, "That's who I am. Now, do you accept? How badly do you want to save your family's building?"

"I wouldn't be a good assistant for you."

Without batting one eyelash, he asked, "Do you want to sleep with me?"

Flustered, she shook her head. "Absolutely not."

With a smug nod, he said, "Well, then, that makes you perfect."

Chapter Four

Kira smoothed down her sundress and grimaced at her reflection in her bedroom. "This is it."

What a difference a week could make. Last Monday she'd picked up the dogs from the animal rescue, taken them for a walk, and knocked down the CEO of the company looking to raze her mother's legacy. Now he was her boss.

No amount of research and pre-planning had prepared her for the likes of Blake Whitman, challenge gleaming in his light brown eyes. He didn't think she'd do it. He'd taken one look at her frumpy, ill-fitting suit and thrown out a wild offer. Give the girl a job as a secretary. Save a building. No skin off his shoulder. It must be so easy for guys like him to get whatever they wanted whenever they wanted it.

Her father was a perfect example. Work all day, mess with people's lives, and play at night with whoever caught his fancy.

Well, it would serve him right to have to deal with her. She could handle him, and he didn't even know the half of what she was capable of accomplishing. That sweet deal for the strip mall instead of baseball fields for the community park he'd lost last year had been partly her doing. The bid he'd placed for the chain grocery store to go next to the library had been stopped by a petition she'd helped organize.

She knew Blake Whitman, had seen him in action with his arm candy, and the way he'd thrown out the job offer surprised her. That he'd be willing to hire her as his secretary without knowing anything more than her name and the fact she wanted to save a neighborhood. She wondered what his scheme was. Now that she'd be working for him she'd have plenty of time to find out.

Tish stretched across the bed and sipped the last of her breakfast smoothie. "You look like every guy's hot secretary fantasy."

Kira wrinkled her nose. Attracting her multimillionaire boss was not the strategy she wanted to take. Especially since she'd said she didn't want to sleep with him. "Despite whatever fantasies you have about *your* boss, I'm not in the market right now. I'm there to save the building." No matter how hot he was. And damn, was Blake Whitman smoking. But he didn't sleep with secretaries and fired the ones who wanted to sleep with him.

So it didn't matter that Blake's dark hair and dark golden eyes had haunted her since he'd picked up Muffin and cuddled him. She'd always been a sucker for tall, dark, and handsome, and the fact that her new boss was dog-friendly, too, only added to the interest in him she didn't want to have.

She still couldn't believe Tish had convinced her to confront Blake. Now, she had a great paying job and The Bromwell Building might be saved without getting her dad involved, assuming her boss followed through with his end of the deal. Lucky for her, she'd be working for him, and she could follow-up with his promise to entertain other design options.

Tish rolled her eyes. "Why didn't you tell your dad?"

"My dad said real estate wasn't in his wheelhouse, and that if I wanted, he'd find me another building. He never felt any attachment in the same way I did and complained about the upkeep and money spent on refurbishments. It's not just the building for me."

She grabbed a blazer and buttoned it over the sundress.

After nodding her approval, her friend exited the room as she said, "I know. We'll make this work without your dad."

Kira sighed and took one last stare at herself in the mirror. Until yesterday, she hadn't worn a blazer in a year, but that year felt like it happened a different lifetime ago. Back before she figured out that life wasn't a sprint, and she didn't want to be first.

She didn't deny she earned her JD-MBA to please her father, but it was her mother's journal he'd given her just before graduation that changed her attitude about what it meant to be successful. So many charities needed capable volunteers and there weren't enough hours in the day to do everything. After a year working endless hours for her father's consulting company, she felt like she wasn't connecting with the corporate life or doing much good for the community. She'd had a serious discussion with him about her interest in spending more time on the community revitalization efforts to continue her mom's vision of creating historic Edgewater Bay.

It terrified her to have a tiny bubble of excitement brewing in her gut at working for a big corporation again. No way would she allow the adrenaline of a new job to make her feel like a sellout. This time would be different. She'd have a charity allowance, money to devote toward local projects, and as Blake said, she'd have a chance to be part of the solution. She'd be there when the board voted on which plans to approve, and she'd probably have a louder voice if she was someone on the inside.

"Are you ready?" Tish leaned her perfectly French-braided head into the doorframe.

Ready to return to an office. Ready to face her new boss. Taking a deep breath, she exhaled slowly. *Mellow. Think mellow.*

Kira followed her friend to the kitchen and after refilling the water and food bowls, opened a doggy crate for their latest foster puppy to hop inside. This one, a malnourished Maltese mix, strolled into the cushioned crate, wandered in a circle a couple of times, and then curled into a ball. Kira latched the baby gate separating the kitchen from the rest of the apartment.

"See you at lunch, Coconut."

When she realized her humans were leaving, Coconut scrambled off the cushion and gave a mournful howl. Kira shot Tish a desperate stare. "We can't leave her."

The dog yelped and scrambled at the gate.

Kira shook her head. "No. I'm not leaving her here." The Maltese needed to be fed every couple of hours, and leaving her in the crate until lunch would be cruel. With a sick knot in her gut, she ran to her room to find a large tote. Blake would be fine with Coconut. He had to be. He liked dogs and had picked the animal shelter for his charity donations.

With the dog safely tucked into the tote over Kira's shoulder, Tish grabbed the water bowl and formula. "I have morning meetings, but maybe if you hide her under your desk, I can take her in the afternoon."

Once in Tish's reliable silver sedan, Kira leaned her head back and gently caressed Coconut to calm her. "I need another coffee."

Ironic really, after chastising Blake for his caffeine consumption.

"I'll make you one at the office."

She laughed. "Shouldn't I be the one to offer you coffee?

You know, since I'm a secretary." She lowered the visor and stared at her reflection for the millionth time. Since when had she turned so vain? "Need to get into character," she muttered.

"No one will expect you to make coffee. You're not that kind of secretary."

"Oh my gawd, there are different kinds of secretaries?" She'd never had a secretary, but she was pretty sure her dad's made him coffee every morning. Perhaps she really didn't know what she was doing.

"I meant the kind in the 1950s."

Heat flushed up Kira's neck, as she imagined herself as a 1950s secretary, complete with steno pad and pencil, awaiting Blake's dictation. Was that why she was so nervous? Why her stomach wouldn't calm down? Because in less than ten minutes she would embark on a new adventure that would place her directly in the man's path for twelve months? "What kind of secretary will I be?" she wondered out loud.

"A good one. You're such a perfectionist, you won't fail."

Kira stared out the window, too shocked to respond to Tish's too close to home insinuation. She watched the people on the newly widened pathway approved by the City Council last spring, the freshly painted signs over the strip malls as they whizzed by, and the unprecedented number of out-of-town license plates from tourists.

Anything to distract her from the real issues. Like how she'd woken in a slight panic over taking a job much more tedious than the one she'd left, and would her father lecture her when he found out, and she'd never had a secretary nor had she ever been one, so what if she didn't know what she was doing? She sucked in her breath. This wasn't the time for her to start second-guessing herself.

Blake had put it perfectly when he'd offered her the job.

Work for him for one year and save her mom's vision.

Preserve not only the landmark building but also the entire tract of that neighborhood. A weird bargain—especially because he didn't seem to care what qualifications she had—but maybe he thought he could work her to the bone, drive her to quit in a week, then do what he wanted with the Bromwell.

Well, he'd met his match, because no matter how demanding he was, she'd deal with whatever he threw at her, spend his company's money on charitable projects, and save the community.

Starting this job was not a defining moment in her life, anyway. It was like any other job she'd taken in the past year and a half, and not a step on the corporate career ladder. A volunteer effort to save the livelihoods of countless people and preserve the neighborhood. So what if she wanted to be competent at it?

Finally she mumbled, "I'm not a perfectionist."

"Whatever you say." Tish's tone was laced with sarcasm.

They rode into the building's parking garage in silence. Coconut perked up the moment the car stopped, and Kira tucked the dog into the tote, following Tish to the elevator.

As they waited, Kira reached into the tote and stroked Coconut's head. "Good girl. We're going to have a great day. Nothing we can't handle, right?"

"Are you petting your purse?" The deep baritone caught her off guard, and she whirled around to face her new boss.

The elevator doors dinged open and she rushed inside, slipping the tote from her shoulder to hang between the wall and the side of her legs. Tish stepped in front, as if trying to form a barrier between them. "Good morning, Blake."

Despite the initial shock, Kira kept her voice calm. "Coconut is malnourished and you didn't say dogs weren't allowed."

His gaze dropped to her tote. Warmth spread up Kira's neck as she noted that he stared a bit longer than a quick look, and that what probably caught his attention were her shoes.

Stilettos, really. Black, high, and with a royal blue bow tied right at her Achilles' heel. They matched the print on her sundress perfectly, and with the blazer her friend suggested, the outfit screamed uptight but sexy, a contradiction that worked well with her warring emotions. Not that she was trying for sexy, the outfit was one that she'd felt confident in — and she needed all the confidence she could muster.

As soon as Blake entered the elevator, she caught a whiff of delicious male scent that lingered in the back of her throat and made her mouth water. Even as she told herself to calm down, that it was just soap and maybe aftershave, she still leaned slightly into him and inhaled. Something triggered her brain to alert her body that a super hot male stood near her, and her skin tingled to life. He smelled too damn good, and a wave of uncertainty sprinkled over her.

What if she fell for her boss?

He focused on her face, and she heard his incredulity when he said, "Truthfully, bringing a pet to work never crossed my mind."

"She won't be a hassle. I'll keep her under my desk. I'd already committed to fostering her. I have to feed her every two hours and I couldn't leave her at home. I promise she won't be a disruption." Kira's fingers tightened around the tote's strap. "You won't even know she's there."

He looked down and then back up again. With that tilted grin she'd seen several times already, he said, "Oh, I doubt that." He cocked his head to the side and studied her. "Tell me…did you bring a crate?"

Of all the irresponsible actions Kira could claim, forgetting about the crate had to be at the top of the list. She hadn't given much thought to how she'd contain Coconut, thinking to tie her leash to the desk or something. "I don't need one."

He turned to her roommate. "Perhaps you could show Kira where to find an empty copy paper box."

Kira blew out a breath. "So it's okay? It's fine that Coconut is here?"

"Let's see how today goes, okay?"

At least she didn't have to take the dog home. A rush of relief flowed from her. "Thank you. Thank you so much. I promise, you won't even know she's here." She placed her free hand on his arm and felt the muscle under her palm tense. He kept a reserved expression on his face, and she hadn't meant anything more than gratitude when she'd touched him, but she jerked her arm back and clamped her lips closed. No way did she want him to think she was coming onto him. "I-I didn't mean—"

He nodded. "No problem."

The elevator doors dinged open, and Kira entered the open reception area. Tish turned and hugged her, breaking the awkward moment. "I'll find you for lunch, okay?"

"Yes. Lunch." She glanced back at Blake. "Do I get lunch?"

Blake frowned. "Of course you get lunch."

Tish left and Kira turned to Blake. "Where would you like me, sir?" There. That should redraw the line. Let him know she viewed him as her supervisor and not some sexy piece of manhood she'd like to— She coughed. Really, she usually had much better control over her thoughts.

His lips pressed into a thin line then he said, "Follow me."

The fourth floor layout was one open concept with low-rise cubicles. Offices lined the outer walls, and the spacious room allowed Kira to see from the bank of elevators to the far end of the building with little obstruction. He led her down a different path than the one Tish took, and it surprised her to hear how many people Blake greeted by name. In her dad's office, she could walk by a dozen people and though she recognized their faces, she didn't know anything about them. But here, he knew their name, asked them personal questions, and though he kept pace as they headed toward his office, she could tell the people here were friendly.

In an attempt to make light conversation and maybe connect with her new boss, she said, "Tish and I foster dogs through the same animal rescue that you sometimes support."

"That's admirable."

"It would be great if you could contribute regularly."

He shot her a smile that stalled her mid-thought. "First hour here and already trying to get money from me?"

"Oh, sir. I didn't—"

He let out a small chuckle. "I'm messing with you."

"Not funny." But Kira hid her smile. No sense letting him know she liked his teasing.

He placed a hand over his heart but continued walking. "My apologies."

When he stopped in front of a door marked with his name, she noticed the large, L-shaped desk guarding said door.

"Nice digs. Is this where I'll be?"

"Yes. Make yourself at home."

"At work."

"Excuse me?"

"I'll make myself at work. Since, you know, this isn't my home."

He chuckled, but Kira couldn't tell if he thought her quip was amusing or if he was just laughing at her. "I'll give you ten minutes to get Coconut settled, and then let's meet in my office."

"Okay." Ten minutes to poke around and make a list of the potential questions and supplies she'd need. "Ten minutes. Do I knock or is there an intercom system?"

"Just walk in. Like you did yesterday."

If only that sounded as welcoming as she wanted it to be.

Chapter Five

From where he sat, Blake could glimpse Kira as she clipped Coconut into her leash and wound it around the foot of the desk. Though he couldn't make out what she said to the dog, her tone sounded soothing.

He snorted. What kind of woman would bring a dog to work on her first day and think it would be acceptable? The kind he tricked into hiring, obviously. As he tried to avoid noting the distractingly enticing curve of her calf, he couldn't shake the feeling that things might get complicated.

The phone rang, and several things happened at once to prove his concern. As Kira scooted out from under the desk, her dress lifted to reveal a thin strip of electric blue lace barely covering her ass, and when she lifted the phone and answered, "Blake Whitman's office. How may I help you?" the phone continued to ring. She turned to face him, a bewildered expression on her face as she brushed back dark hair that had tumbled loose from her braid, and he knew he'd been caught staring at her with a slack jaw. He didn't care.

Still, that image of her would take days to shake off.

Dark hair mussed, face flushed, and that thong. He couldn't look her in the eye, even from across the room. He'd spent a lifetime brushing off silly females wanting something from him, and now he'd put in his way the one female who sparked his interest, who he couldn't have because he'd offered her a position guaranteed to keep her off limits to him. He'd never considered himself a masochist.

Damn he was in trouble.

Grabbing the phone, he barked, "Keith, I'm in the middle of something." *Losing my common sense.* "So this better be urgent."

His brother's jovial tone irritated him more than usual. "When are you not in the middle of something? Anyway, I just wanted to confirm the rumor that you hired a hot secretary."

Hot. Kira was definitely hot. The comment rattled Blake's nerves and he lied, "She's not hot."

She was breathtakingly beautiful. His body had been on high alert since he'd stood next to her in the elevator, and he didn't think he'd ever needed to exert so much energy on not noticing a woman before.

In the space of several heartbeats, he could concoct a whole slew of reasons to call this whole farce off, but in the center of his silent debate were Kira's soft brown eyes begging him to save her mom's building. *Really?* Since when had he gone soft? But he hadn't offered her the job because of pity.

No. He'd offered because he'd been bored.

She'd come at him through all his senses, at the right time and saying the right things, and in the week since he'd last seen her, he hadn't second-guessed himself once. Now, staring at the sharp length of her heels, he could think of a million things he'd rather have her do than work for him for a year.

The line went dead and Blake frowned, on the verge of calling back his brother when he eyed Kira standing in his doorway. The woman was downright distracting.

She held her hands behind her, and his gaze landed on her chest. He closed his eyes. Maybe because they'd met under unusual circumstances, he had difficulty classifying her as an employee. His secretary.

With a shy but playful grin, she said, "Sorry to interrupt, but you said to just walk in."

He looked at the receiver, couldn't remember whom he was trying to call, and replaced it in the cradle. After clearing his throat, he gestured for her to take the chair opposite his desk. "Yes. Of course."

As she advanced into the room, she unbuttoned her blazer. "I'm a little warm. Mind if I take this off so I don't get hot?" *Hot.* Had she heard what he'd said to his brother? If she was trying to get a reaction out of him, it wouldn't work. Over the years, he'd perfected the poker face. He shrugged. "Whatever makes you comfortable."

"Thank you."

She slid out of the blazer, and though the sundress certainly could be considered modest at the neckline, her bare shoulders covered with thin spaghetti straps caught his attention. She gave the jacket a gentle shake then folded it, and he breathed in a whiff of sweet perfume. The temperature in the room rose a thousand degrees, and he resisted the urge to loosen his tie. Other employees had tried to distract him, but none had ever succeeded. In a matter of minutes, Kira had managed to wiggle her way into the front of his thoughts. It stunned him.

He just had to keep reminding himself she was here because she wanted something from him, so she really was no different than any other woman who had breezed through his life.

He went on the offensive to ground himself. "I noticed you had difficulty answering the phone. I'll ask Darcy, my brother's assistant, to train you. I know the multiple lines might seem complicated, but I'm sure you won't have any trouble once you grasp the basics."

Her boss thought she was an idiot.

As if overhearing him say she wasn't hot hadn't been enough of a blow to her ego, the sincerity in his expression about having someone train her on how to use a phone hit the point home. It seemed like he really meant it when he said multiple lines might be complicated, and if she hadn't been embarrassed about having her skirt catch on the under-desk drawer earlier, she probably would have hit the right line and answered correctly the first time. But she'd felt the breeze, and as soon as she saw his face, she knew she'd flashed him.

"I'm sure I can figure it out."

"Someone from IT should be by in about an hour to show you our computer system. Maybe that's a good time for Darcy to train you on the phones and email. She can also take you to the inventory room for supplies. I don't suppose you brought a notepad and pen in here with you?" Kira opened her mouth, but the phone rang again. Without hesitating, she hopped up and skipped around to Blake's side of the desk. This time she pushed the flashing button before she said, "Blake Whitman's office. How may I assist you?"

"This is Keith. Is this Kira?"

"Yes, Keith. Would you like to hold for Blake?" She turned to him, and her thoughts stalled when she saw how close to him she actually stood, and how his gaze seemed to be riveted on her feet. She sidestepped and his head moved just slightly. Yup. The guy was a shoe man.

"Sir?" She wiggled the phone in front of him. "Keith is on the line for you."

"My brother. I'll introduce you." He took the phone.

"I thought you'd be in here by now." Then he hung up and pointed to the open door. "Wait for it."

She continued to stand on his side of the desk and looked out into the open space. The door at the opposite end of the large office area opened and a man exited, making a beeline toward Blake's office.

"This is my brother, Keith. He's the VP."

Keith entered, a huge smile on his face. "I'm pleased to meet you. I hope you'll find it rewarding to work here at Whitman-Madison."

She stepped around the desk and shook his outstretched hand. "I'm looking forward to it."

"Has Blake reviewed the employee contract with you yet?"

She chewed on her lower lip and then released it. Bad habit, but one she'd been trying to break. "Not yet."

"Well, it's pretty standard." To Blake he said, "I'll send Darcy over. She can walk Kira around. Show her downstairs, too."

"And phones," Kira couldn't help saying as she shot her boss an innocent smile. "I think I need Darcy to train me on answering phones."

Kira hated how her body reacted to Blake. It was quarter to six, and she'd decided to stay put until Blake returned from a three o'clock meeting on the third floor. She'd spent the day arranging her desk, feeding Coconut, and setting up her email account.

Finally he was back, and they were alone in his office. She sat across the desk from him, and her gaze lingered on his chest as he removed his jacket and rolled his shirtsleeves. She opened her notebook and rattled off the first of twelve messages, stopping to appreciate the way he loosened his tie and unbuttoned his top button. She stared at his forearms, corded with muscle and a faint smattering of dark hair, and despite her desire to appear competent and focused, she couldn't rip her gaze from his strong hands.

"Kira?"

His tone broke through her haze of hormones, and she blinked down at her notes. "Bobby called regarding a barbecue restaurant, and he said it's not a problem if you call him after hours." She placed a neat check mark in the margin and handed him a file folder. "I hope you don't mind, but I searched your files and pulled this for your reference. There's a sticky note on the page he wants to discuss."

He took the folder. "Not a problem."

She nodded. "Good. I was worried you'd think I was snooping."

"For doing your job? Not at all." He placed the folder to the side. "Next?"

"Michelle Paul called to confirm lunch tomorrow, and she prefers the Seed to Table place over the, and I quote, last joint you chose."

Blake laughed, drawing her attention to his jaw, where she could see the evening stubble. How any man could capture her attention so completely baffled her, and she really hoped it was the novelty of their situation that intrigued her. She wanted to stand there and stare at the man all day, maybe even taste him…

He rubbed the back of his neck. "What else?"

For the briefest moment, his gaze collided with hers and her pulse quickened. Could he tell she basically wanted to recant her earlier animosity against him? After all, what girl could resist the guy giving her everything she wanted?

She'd read a memo in his email that he'd sent himself on the urban design for historic areas, which had prompted her to research the benefits of walkable towns and green space. He'd also asked her to provide a list of possible charities for him to support, demonstrating he hadn't forgotten his offer to give her an allowance from his personal funds.

She'd been so elated she could have kissed him, if he'd been around, and it was probably a good thing that he hadn't been.

"I saw the email you sent earlier. I wanted to thank you, for allowing me the opportunity to really make a difference with your money."

His eyes crinkled in a smile. "You're not the first woman to offer to spend my money, but at least I know you'll spend it wisely."

Good, old-fashioned curiosity had her wondering what other women he was talking about and how many? She hoped he didn't think she was using him, but they'd been clear from the start. Secretary. Building. She needed to get it together.

"You also have a note regarding my contract," she reminded him.

"Yes." He dug through his desk drawer and then held out a slim folder. "Why don't you pull over a chair, and we'll go through it. Of course, you should take it home and review it at your leisure, but I'd like to address the main points together, if you have time."

They spent the next hour reviewing the twelve-page document detailing her employment conditions. Wages, confidentiality agreement, non-compete clause, social media usage, and benefits. She didn't have an issue with any of it. The terms were standard, and she wouldn't have a problem complying with any of the clauses.

She didn't need to take it home. She signed. He signed. They closed the contract, and then he moved away from her.

He cleared his throat. "This is going to sound awkward, but it's better if we clarify this from the beginning."

She glanced toward his office door, a sinking feeling in her stomach. He was going to tell her Coconut couldn't come back, and she'd have to hate him. Stuck in another office for a year, unable to foster any animals. Maybe if she showed him a journal article discussing the merits of animals and lower blood pressure...

He lowered his voice. "Privacy laws restrict an employer from prohibiting employee relationships, but it's best to be clear that I stand against workplace dating."

Against. Workplace. Dating. It took her brain a full minute to digest that he wasn't kicking out her foster. She'd already said she didn't want to sleep with him. "So I can keep Coconut?"

He raised his brows. "The dog is fine. Did you hear what I said?"

She could hug him for letting her keep Coconut. She uncrossed her legs and slowly rose. "We had the"—she made air quotes—"'are you attracted to me?' discussion before you offered me the position. I assure you, you have nothing to worry about where I'm concerned."

He scrubbed his hair back from his forehead, even as he glanced at her shoes. "That's a relief."

Even though it was what they both wanted, his reaction bothered her.

After a glance at the clock, he opened his wallet and extracted a couple bills. "Hungry? How about we raid the vending machine? I'll show you where it is."

As he followed her out of his office, she dropped the messages on her desk and poked her head underneath to check on Coconut. The dog, clearly in the middle of an active dream, didn't even acknowledge her presence.

"Stairs?" Kira pushed through the door before Blake could hit the elevator button, and as he brushed by her, she inhaled an intoxicating amount of male. Even after a long day, he smelled fresh and warm and delicious.

Against workplace dating.

That's what he'd said, and it was what she needed to remember.

His cell phone rang, echoing loudly in the stairwell. She tried to not listen, but the woman on the other end spoke with crystal clarity. His neck flushed, and he looked like he was one step away from slamming the phone against the wall.

The way his body moved, prowled down the stairs, really, had her fantasizing about him whirling on her and pressing her against the wall.

Wow. Since when did she daydream sexual fantasies? Here she was, acting as a secretary and pretending to not want to jump her boss after hours. If only her classmates could see her now. They'd joked about how she'd be the CEO before any of them, considering her connections and her six-figure salary straight out of graduate school.

Blake's reiteration of the unwritten no-fraternization clause was a good reminder that she was here only for a year. For the Bromwell and for the community. No matter how hot her boss was, there was no crossing that line or the entire historic area would be torn down and replaced with sleek high rises and modern shopping malls devoid of charm, catering to the stream of high-end tourists. She'd seen long-time residents forced from their neighborhoods all over this area of Florida and refused to let it happen here. As much as she entertained the idea of a fling, the man wasn't worth it.

As Blake led them through the third floor's lobby and into the employees only lounge, he ended the call and slid the phone in his pocket, drawing her attention to that area of his pants. Again her brain left logic at the curb and sped toward inappropriate imaginings.

He sighed audibly when they reached the vending machines. "Ah, chocolate. Just what I need."

Chocolate would barely satisfy what Kira needed, but it would have to do. As his fingers inserted the bill in the machine, she imagined him dragging those fingers over her body. She swallowed.

What the hell was the matter with her? A small giggle escaped. She covered both hands over her mouth and stared at him, waiting for him to say something.

His eyebrows shot up. "Something funny?"

She shook her head. "I think my blood sugar must be low. Good thing you thought to get us a snack."

His gaze stayed on her for a long moment and her entire body whipped to life, silently begging him to like what he saw. Had he been pleased with his day? Did it turn out the way he wanted? Did he think she'd be an okay secretary for him?

Finally, he said, "And we get to do it all again tomorrow."

Chapter Six

"No, Coconut. Bad."

Kira hopped up from her desk and rushed into Blake's office. "What? What's wrong?" She'd survived her first full week, and this morning they'd shared a celebratory coffee from The Fresh Bean.

"Your damn dog was climbing up my leg. Again."

She crouched on the floor by his chair and caressed the top of the Maltese's head. "Awwww. She likes you. Probably just wanted to cuddle." To Coconut, Kira used her baby-talk tone. "Isn't that right, Coco, just cuddle?" Glancing up at Blake, she grinned into his frown. "Admit it, you're going to miss her next week." And then scooted back when she realized just how close to his thigh she'd gotten.

"She won't be here next week?"

Heat rose on her cheeks as she spun back to focus on Coconut, ignoring the impressive bulge she noticed behind his zipper. What had she been thinking, sinking to the floor at his feet? "I'm going to pretend you don't sound relieved about that."

"What happened? Did she find a family?"

"The Edgewater Animal Rescue rotates the dogs every week." With her back still to Blake, she sank back to her butt and pulled Coconut into her lap. "So next week we won't have her. She'll be at the shelter."

"Why?"

At the genuine curiosity in his voice, she looked over her shoulder at his face—focused on just his face—and as she absently rubbed the dog's head, she also noticed how he'd put down the tablet and focused on her. "You really want to know?"

"I wouldn't have asked otherwise."

"There aren't enough foster families to house all the dogs, and this way each dog gets rotated to a home for individual attention. It helps with the newly abandoned dogs to have more human contact."

"Smart idea."

The way he listened and didn't laugh at her for being invested in animal foster care almost made her forget the long hours he'd made her put in this week. Good thing he'd let her keep the dog at work, because if not, Coconut would end up staying crated for too many hours, in which case the shelter would be the better option.

She grinned up at him. "It's a great rescue."

He surprised her by slipping out of his chair and joining her on the floor. "I asked my accountant to get in touch with you next week. He'll give you a list of where I currently donate, and I told him you get twenty percent to distribute for next year's contributions." When Coconut stretched her legs to touch Blake, he grabbed a paw and shook it. "Like for the animal rescue."

"That's so fantastic. I'll print out the documentation for monthly sponsors. It will help so much!"

"Does losing Coconut mean we'll have another beast in here next week?"

Something squeezed in Kira's chest. He really was okay with the foster dogs in the office. Other staff had asked about the program, but not too many employees had pets at home. Kira respected that they knew their limitations, and with most everyone working either long days or irregular hours, pets didn't exactly fit into their lifestyle.

"I told the placement coordinator that I wasn't sure if I could keep fostering, but if you're okay with it?"

When his computer dinged, he released Coconut and settled back into his chair. As he checked his email, with his back to her, he said, "I survived this week, didn't I? Go ahead and bring in the next victim. Maybe as long as it's small?"

She stared at his rigid back and the way his dark hair just barely brushed over his crisp collar. He might work ninety hours a week, and maybe he'd fired more than one employee for not being able to keep up with his rigorous standards, but she understood why some of her predecessors wanted more than a working relationship. She couldn't blame them. This Blake, the one who took a couple minutes to pet a homeless dog, threatened her equilibrium.

"Don't take this the wrong way, but right now I could kiss you."

Blake choked back the image of his lips covering Kira's and said, "Uh. Thank you?"

She must have sensed she'd irritated him, because she skipped around to the front of the desk and clarified, "Appropriately, of course, and it's not like I'd really kiss you. I mean." Her eyes widened. "I only meant—um—thank you. Thank you again for being so generous."

His mouth curved into a frown, but his body responded to her flirtation about rewarding him with *appropriate* kisses for letting her foster. He picked up his tablet and swiped back to the email from the architect. However she'd meant it, he now had an image of her kissing him, and he waited until she'd backed out of his office before swiveling around to stare out the window at the bay. He glanced at the horizon, trying to remember the last time he'd been so distracted.

He'd never had a secretary he couldn't figure out, and because she'd only taken the job to influence the decision of the downtown plans, he couldn't fit her into a neat box labeled, "Secretary." Not when she left him brilliant comments on pink sticky notes referencing clients and follow-up conference calls.

The dog had been a surprise, but people in the office responded well, and other than leaving her desk to walk Coconut, the animal didn't disrupt his work day much. She had also made sure to email him medical journal studies in which pets were shown to lower stress and blood pressure in patients. Crafty girl.

Not that he was complaining. He could handle the tiny beast.

What he wasn't sure he could handle was his imagination. Every day since the first one, he'd stared at her shoes and then her ass, wondering if her panties matched her stilettos like they had that first day. He really shouldn't be looking at her like that, but the pesky memory kept resurfacing at the worse damn times, torturing him by replaying how her skirt had lifted to reveal the strip of electric blue thong that perfectly matched the bows tied around her ankles.

He had a million and ten demanding issues that needed his attention, including how she'd just roped him into participating in the Edgewater Animal Rescue foster program.

Now, not only would he contribute funds on a monthly basis to support the rescue, but he'd agreed to have different dogs delivered to his office every week. While he happened to love animals, he wondered who would save his jaded ass from the young woman with doe-brown eyes and plump lips he'd like to feast upon.

He didn't date in the workplace, but lately he hadn't dated anywhere. That had to be the reason Kira caught his attention.

He risked a sideways glance to see if she was at her desk and caught her reading her email, her legs crossed, the heel of one shoe dangling from her toe. Damn sexy. What he wouldn't give to have those legs wrapped around his hips. But he wasn't supposed to be thinking about her like that. Even if the sight of her bare legs made him forget he wasn't a teenager.

She arched back, stretching provocatively. Her shoe fell from her toe, and as she bent to retrieve it, the chair slid out from under her. Landing with a soft thud and a quiet laugh, she turned and caught him staring at her. Neither of them moved for what seemed like an eternity, and he couldn't look away from the light in her dark eyes.

She broke their eye contact first, and as she slipped on her shoe and regained her seat, he picked up the file on his desk. She'd wasted no time organizing his folders and commandeering his calendar. The girl had savvy written all over her, and although he hadn't known anything about her when he'd offered her the job, she'd more than proven she was exactly what Keith had in mind when he said to hire a secretary who would stick around, focus on work, and not want to sleep with him.

Part of her intrigue had to be her commitment to preserving the downtown area. In order to save a building, she'd been willing to sign away a year of her life. He couldn't help it. He admired her.

Too bad he couldn't claim the same kind of self-control. He still couldn't believe he'd suggested the arrangement so spontaneously. But, he'd always been focused on expanding the investments his grandfather had started and never before had he allowed a woman to take precedence over the company's bottom line. Apparently, he'd hired the only woman able to capture his interest in a long while.

His computer dinged. Lunch meeting with Christopher Harlowe to discuss a new software integration system for their law firm, which gave him a great idea.

Grabbing his wallet from the drawer, he shoved his sunglasses to the top of his head and grinned like a teenager in lust. His reaction was ridiculous, but there it was. She made him want to forget about work for even the briefest of moments and just—be.

"Kira?"

"Sir?"

Call him egotistical, but he loved when she called him sir. "I'm heading out to a business lunch. I'd like you to join me."

Her face brightened. "Really?" She sounded so damn excited. She stood and smoothed her hands down her lean frame, accentuating the curves under her sundress. "Let me put Coconut in Tish's office." She moved out of his office, and he followed her.

Damn his stupid libido and his rash invitation. He didn't need her there, but Kira already had Coconut in her arms, her purse over her shoulder, and that excited smile on her mouth.

Her roommate took the dog without question. Then, Kira and he caught the elevator before he could change his mind.

She followed him to the parking lot. "This is so exciting."

"It's lunch." He hoped he hadn't made a mistake in leading her to think this was anything but a meal with a vendor. But he'd wanted to spend more time with her, and just because he'd never done it in the past, didn't mean it was abnormal for him to invite his secretary to a business lunch.

"Yes. I love lunch." She hopped in the passenger seat and clicked into her seat belt, the strap snugly outlining her breasts. "Where are we going? It wasn't marked on your calendar."

A dozen inappropriate answers flew to the tip of his tongue. He choked them back and said, "Limoncello's," naming the exclusive restaurant.

"I love that place! Do you need me to take notes?"

He could feel her looking at him, but he kept his gaze on the road and not on her bare calves.

"Mostly it's networking. Christopher Harlowe is the new kid on the technology block. We're interested in his integration software for our medical center." Given his limitations regarding technology, Blake didn't go into further detail.

"The one on Palm Street?"

She'd definitely done her research on his current projects. Impressive.

In his peripheral vision, he noticed her twist toward him, and when she tucked one leg under the other, her flimsy dress rose farther up her thigh. "So you don't really need me?"

The light scent of her perfume lingered in his brain, along with the quick glimpse he caught of her smooth thigh now burning the sexy image into his memory. He forced his gaze forward, driving a little more recklessly than usual in order to get them out of the confines of the SUV. He hadn't anticipated the close proximity sharing a vehicle would entail. It would be so easy for him to stretch his hand and touch her bare skin.

His grip tightened on the steering wheel. "No, I need you."

She swallowed loud enough for him to hear. Had she misinterpreted that remark? He could mean it so many different ways. Okay, two different ways. But he didn't. Mean it. Like that. He had to clarify.

"Kira." He meant to say her name as a warning, but it came out sounding like a plea.

"What?" Her innocent tone caught him in the gut every damn time, and he couldn't leave her alone. She'd told him from the start that she wasn't interested, so why did he view that as a challenge?

What was the matter with him? He never mixed work with pleasure, and they had a contract stating she'd be his employee for one year. She was forbidden fruit. Other coworkers had dated and broken up across different departments without bringing serious drama to work, but Blake never risked it. He'd never wanted to risk it.

He reminded himself she was only interested in him for what his company could do for her, anyway. "I'm bringing you along because I'm interested in your impression of this potential vendor. You're sharp, you've done great work this week, and you've got good instincts. Just make notes of any questions that come up along the way."

The heat from the Floridian sun baked the car. He opened his door, hot and anxious to put some space between them.

Slipping from the car, she said, "Oh. Thank you."

She sashayed around the back of the SUV, the cutest wrinkle in her nose.

A warning shot straight to his gut, like he'd just left Pandora's box unlocked, but these unused emotions intrigued him, and he was curious. Shoving aside his inappropriate thoughts, he matched her step as they approached the restaurant. He knew the exact moment Christopher Harlowe spotted them. The man licked his lips, his gaze so obviously on Kira's long legs, that Blake instinctively stepped in front of her, blocking her from Christopher's view.

The man shook his hand but made no effort to hide his interest in Kira. "Hi, I'm Christopher."

"Hello. I'm Kira." Her voice sounded half an octave lower and slightly on the formal side. "It's a pleasure to meet you."

Blake glanced over his shoulder to see his secretary, her mouth closed in a tight-lipped smile. Gone was her flirty demeanor.

For some reason, one he wasn't ready to explore, this pleased him immensely.

Chapter Seven

"Why didn't you silence your phone?" Tish hissed as Kira dug around her oversized bag for the source of the interruption.

"I did." Or at least she thought she had. It shouldn't have mattered. The only people she usually hung around on a Sunday night were sitting in the movie theater with her. No one actually called her phone anymore, not even her father. So the obnoxiously repetitive old rotary dial ring had to be a wrong number.

When she finally located the phone, she clicked it silent and then stared in disbelief at the number she'd just ignored.

Blake Whitman.

To say her pulse sped up was an understatement, and that was followed by annoyance at her body betraying her. Once again, just the thought of Blake had her imagining how she'd entice him if they'd met under any other circumstances. But she attended events as a volunteer, and he attended as a table sponsor.

No matter her personal feelings, she wanted him to know

he could rely on her—for at least a year. After all, if he was making the serious effort to preserve the downtown area, then she would make the same level of commitment to her secretarial position.

By the time she reached the lobby, her phone chimed again with a voicemail notification.

"Kira, I know it's Sunday night, but please call my cell if you have time. It's not really work-related. Otherwise, I'll see you in the morning."

Well, that wasn't too cryptic. Instinct had her dialing his number, since she never could turn away from someone asking for her help, but when it rang, she heard the double beep indicating he was on the other line, and left a message. Finally, a text came through.

Thanks for calling back. Sorry I missed you. All is well. Pic to follow.

The next message showed Blake holding a chocolate Labrador with a cast on its front paw.

Her heart squeezed at the image, and she swallowed the giant lump of feelings in her throat as she texted him back.

Awww, so cute. What happened?

Hit and run by hospital. Didn't know where to take him. Nurse gave me address to emergency vet.

Do you need me to come get him?

I'm good. We're still here.

Text me the address. I'll be there in a bit.

Damn Blake and his hit-and-run rescue. She'd spent the weekend keeping busy, trying to keep her mind from wandering to her boss. One text message, and she understood how those other secretaries—the ones he'd fired for getting too close—had fallen under his spell. And if she didn't stay on the straight and narrow for a year, he'd fire her. She couldn't just throw herself at him or she'd never save the building and lose those extra dollars toward funding her favorite charities.

And those were the last things she wanted to lose. Still… She texted Tish.

I have to go.

What? Why? Blake?

It's all good. I'll grab a cab. Text me later.

Kira rushed outside and moved toward Restaurant Row of the Edgewater Town Center. The place was packed for a Sunday night, and she couldn't help but notice how popular the trendy town center was. Was that what the city council intended when they voted to redo the downtown area by the bay?

How on earth did she plan to save an entire district, when this was child's play to the Whitman-Madison executives? She studied the town center shaped in a quadrant with restaurants on one side, shops on the other, and the movie theater and pavilion bookending the area—this required board approval and millions of dollars.

For the first time, she questioned Blake's motives for agreeing to go to bat for her building. Maybe it was just a game to him, like hiring a secretary who'd come without qualifications or recommendations.

The cabs lined the side of the street, and she moved to

the front one and instructed the driver to take her to the emergency vet clinic. In the fifteen minutes it took the cabbie to cross town, she reapplied her lip gloss and ran her fingers through her hair. The outfit screamed girls' night, but she couldn't do much to change from the fitted miniskirt and threadbare deep *V* neck tee shirt that had the word LIVE scrawled across her chest.

Blake sat on the wooden bench in the waiting room, with his elbows on his thighs and his head balanced on his clasped hands. She'd never seen him in casual clothes. Slightly rumpled in an untucked navy polo shirt, plaid Bermuda shorts, and boat shoes, he stopped her in her tracks. All she could imagine was a guy she could take to the park and throw a Frisbee with or hop on a boat for an afternoon joyride over the Gulf of Mexico. He looked like…fun.

He glanced up when the door opened, and the raw worry on his face sucker punched Kira in the stomach.

Rushing over to him, she asked, "Any news?"

She saw the surprise in his eyes, but she also saw relief. He'd said she didn't have to come, but no one should wait alone at the doctor's, especially for a dog that wasn't even his. "Thanks for coming."

They spoke at the same time, and Kira pointed for him to go first. "Hit-and-run driver. No collar. But the dog's well-groomed, so they doubt he's a stray. Did you know you can put a chip in your dog?"

"I did." Her mind reeled. How many times would he do something wonderful and how many times would she be caught off guard because of it?

"Thank you for coming." He leaned back and crossed an ankle over his knee.

She stared at his calf, at the smattering of dark hair running up his leg, and wondered if his chest had a little or a lot of hair. Blinking away any yummy images and scolding herself for even thinking about Blake shirtless, she said, "If they don't keep him here, and they can't find his owner, then I'll take him home for the night."

He held up a brochure. "I've got it covered."

She snatched the pamphlet from him. "You do? You'll care for an injured dog based on this trifold?"

He cocked his head and grinned at her, rubbing a hand over the top of his head and leaving it disheveled. She stifled a sigh. The man had a killer smile and when he blinked at her with those honey-colored eyes, her brain stalled and she forgot she wasn't supposed to want him.

"You already have a foster, and I'm guessing it'll be better if this one isn't stressed by another dog." His smile dimmed as his gaze flitted over her, like he just noticed what she was wearing. Heat flushed her chest when he seemed to focus on her cleavage. "Were you on a date?"

It shouldn't matter that he sounded jealous, but something in his tone gave her hope that maybe he wasn't as immune to her as he let on. "Um, no. Would that have mattered?"

He took a long breath. "If you were on a date?"

She tugged up the tee shirt, but the fabric fell back in place, displaying more cleavage than she normally showed at the office. "Yeah. Would you have still called me?"

He shook his head. "If I'd have known you were on a date, I probably wouldn't have bothered you."

She leaned into him and caught the fresh scent of mint. "Probably or wouldn't have?"

"Probably wouldn't have."

She frowned at him. "That's not an answer."

He smiled that killer smile that floored her every damn time.

The doors opened and the veterinarian stepped into the waiting room. "Mr. Whitman? We've repaired the break and sewn up the gash on his neck but would like to keep him here for observation. If you'd like to stop by in the morning, we can update you on his progress."

After answering a few more questions, the vet shook their hands and re-entered the medical area.

Kira turned to Blake. "This was really great, what you did."

He smiled at her with admiration. "You would've done the same thing. Thanks for waiting with me. I'm sorry if I interrupted your evening."

She waved a dismissive hand. "Nothing more important than this. You said you were at the hospital."

They stood facing each other, and up close, even in her heels, she had to lean back to focus on his face. Seeing this softer side of Blake sent her slightly off balance, and she didn't dislike the feeling at all.

"Yes. Visiting a friend."

A male or a female? Curiosity clawed at her, but she clamped down her question. "I was at the movies for girls' night." She watched his expression but couldn't guess his reaction.

"So, not on a date."

"Not on a date." For some reason, she kept thinking of ways to drag out the conversation, and when she realized that was what her brain was doing, she pasted a smile on her face. "Well, I'll see you tomorrow."

"Tomorrow."

She backed out of the clinic and stood on the sidewalk. Really, she needed to go, but she kept saying things, prolonging their interaction. The smart thing to do would be to leave before she said or did something stupid. "I'll pick up coffee on the way in. Do you think you'll need a triple espresso, or will a regular pour be sufficient?"

His smile widened as he scanned the parking lot, empty but for one SUV. "How did you get here. Do you need a ride home?"

"I can get a cab."

"I insist."

She was being ridiculous. A ride was just a ride, not an offer to pleasure her senseless with his curved lips. Her bubble burst with a sharp stab of reality. But damn he looked good, even rumpled.

Kira had to force herself to not invite him inside when his car came to a stop in front of her place. As she closed the gate to her apartment complex and turned to wave, she wondered if she'd made the right choice.

Kira had just placed three thick file folders and a large black coffee on Blake's desk when she heard his luscious baritone outside his office. She spun around and tried to look casual as he entered, his phone in his hand, the Bluetooth in his ear. As soon as he saw her, his face brightened with that captivating smile, and she forgot for a split second—again—that he was her boss.

She mouthed, "Coffee."

He stepped over to claim it, and even after he lifted the lid and sipped, she could smell him—warm and sexy—over the aroma of freshly poured French roast. He spoke to the caller and motioned for Kira to hand him a pad and pen.

"Yes, that's not a problem. I'll have my accountant wire the funds to you this morning."

He tapped his earpiece and tossed it on the desk. "I needed this more than you could possibly know." He sipped and smiled, but his grin dimmed as his gaze lingered on her chest. She'd purposely worn a sundress with a V-neck, and based on the way he licked his lips, he noticed.

She cleared her throat. "You're welcome."

He picked up a folder and opened to the first sticky note she'd tabbed in the margin. After scanning what she'd written, he flipped to the next one, a faint smile curving his mouth. She wondered if she'd gone too far by giving him a running commentary on her assessment of the contracts, but the phones had been eerily silent since she arrived that morning, and she'd decided to read something.

Contradicting her earlier thought, his office line rang. He punched the button and put the caller on speaker. "Brett?"

"It's barely eight on a Monday. Have a little respect for those of us with kids."

Blake's warm laugh filled the office, and she swallowed. The man was lethal, combining his laugh and smile like that. "Brett is my personal accountant." He opened his center drawer and passed her a one-page summary of his investments and charitable contribution deductions.

She scanned the page and leaned forward toward the phone.

"Hello, Kira. Don't let your boss overwork you, too, okay?"

She caught his eye and giggled. "He's already trying to. I think I clocked fifty hours last week."

The accountant made tsk-ing noises. "Just fifty?"

Blake shook his head, but the grin caught her in the gut every damn time. "Let's go ahead and list my current obligations."

Brett rattled off the ones she already knew about, but as he drilled down to the local organizations she wasn't familiar with, she sank back into the chair. Blake contributed anonymously to no less than a dozen organizations.

When the accountant ended his summary, she scooted her seat forward. "Sounds like you've diversified in all the underprivileged areas." Her gaze caught Blake's, and she noticed the dull flush on his neck. The man really was humble.

But she couldn't waste this opportunity to further her own charitable interests. "I'd like to fund my portion of his donations from the interest earned on his vice stocks."

Her boss's slack jaw showed she'd caught him off guard.

Through the phone, the accountant chuckled. "Nicely done, and that total would be"—she heard the clicking of keys—"twenty-six percent of his total in gift contributions."

Blake's eyebrow rose. "That's six percent more than we agreed to." His mouth pursed, then he threw up his hands in defeat and her heart leapt. "Fine."

The more time she spent with the man, the deeper under his spell she fell, but his company had to make money to support his charities; there was no guarantee—short of her contract—that he wouldn't buy the Bromwell and the surrounding buildings for development and use the profits to fund his other interests.

After he hung up, she glanced at her notes. "You volunteer at the veteran's hospital?"

He shrugged. "Once a month."

"And you're going to pay for the dog's medical bills?"

"Brutus. Yes. Until they can find the owner, I'll take care of him." He leaned forward. "Which reminds me. I need to pick up some stuff if I'm going to have a larger dog here. Can you help me?"

"Of course."

He stood and walked by her to the far corner of the room. "I'm thinking we need a small gate to block this section for the dogs. We can see how they get along together, but this way they won't have to be crated." He bent over and slid the coffee table and two armchairs to the side.

She had no words. Just pure lustful appreciation for the way his slacks tightened across his ass. It wasn't fair. It simply wasn't. That the one man to awaken such office fantasies while tugging at her heartstrings was the one man she couldn't have.

"Kira?"

She jerked out of her appreciative trance and blinked up at him. "Yes?"

"What do you think?"

I think you're gorgeous. I think I'd like to wrap my arms around you. She'd like to push him back into the chair and straddle him, nuzzle the side of his face and see if the intoxicating scent was from his aftershave. "I think you're being extraordinarily generous."

A flush crept up his neck. "No big deal."

She'd never met anyone like her boss. For him, it might be nothing, but for her…what seemed insignificant to Blake meant the world to Kira.

"It's not working," Kira groaned, stepping out of her stilettos and dropping her purse to the floor. She'd survived another week, and while most people loved Fridays, to the contrary, leaving the office—leaving Blake—saddened her.

Her roommate made a beeline for the kitchen, returning with two spoons and an open carton of cookies and cream ice cream. "What's not working?"

She tried to hide her frown. "Picturing my boss as a circus clown." Anything to remind her he was off limits. Despite the interest she was certain he had for her, he meant what he said about not mixing business with pleasure.

Against workplace dating.

Tish jabbed her utensil in Kira's direction. "Why on earth would you picture Blake as a clown? Picture him naked if you have to imagine him at all."

She had. Oh, had she ever perfected undressing that man with her eyes. "It's the damn dog."

"I thought you liked Brutus."

She did. She loved Brutus. Unfortunately, she also found herself admiring his rescuer. Saint Blake.

How on earth was she going to survive a year with a hopeless crush on her boss? She groaned. Working for him had sounded like a decent plan when he'd first thrown the idea at her. Why hadn't she asked for more time to make a rational decision? Why had she let emotions get in the way? Save her mom's building, bulk up her bank account, and oh yeah, don't sleep with him.

She had eyeballs. Blake Whitman was super hot, mega rich, and could get any girl he wanted. So why did he suddenly seem like the only guy she wanted to date?

"I do like Brutus. I don't want to like Blake." She admitted her fear. "But that doesn't stop me from creating these elaborate office fantasies."

The corny, over-the-top kind where he would be reviewing a report and she'd saunter in, close the door, and hop onto his desk…

"You need sex. But not with him."

She swiped the carton away from Tish and slapped a giant gob of ice cream into her mouth. Too bad her hot boss was the one guy she wanted to have sex with. "You're probably right."

Tish repossessed the cookies and cream. "When's the last time you went on a date?"

She shrugged. It had been a bunch of months—maybe half a year?—since she'd last gone out with anyone. Her previous boyfriend had been an avid runner, and they'd met while planning a 5K fundraiser. Great stamina. Too bad he'd also been keen on meeting her dad for career opportunities. "Too long, apparently."

Her friend waved her spoon between the two of them. "We're young. We should be out having fun."

"It might have been easier if we'd just met at a bar. Then

maybe we could've hooked up."

"Are you talking about Blake again?"

Tish tossed the spoon in the sink and closed the lid. "No more. But a bar is a great idea!"

"What?" She glanced down at her wrinkled blouse and bare feet.

"It's Friday night. Let's go out."

"To a bar?" Where she'd have to stuff her toes back into pointy heels for the sake of fashion. She scoffed at her dumb brain. Actually, since she'd started working at the office, she'd neglected her own personal party time, and that bothered her more than she wanted to admit. Damn job already had her acting like she was a fuddy duddy.

"Not just any bar. We're going to Tommy Bahamas."

Tish shoved the carton back in the freezer, took the spoon from Kira's hand, and pushed her toward her bedroom. Tommy's did sound fun, and she could count on the bartender to give her a full pour. She recalled seeing Tommy's on Blake's calendar for an early dinner, so even though he might already be gone by the time she got there, excitement mingled with anxiety at potentially running into him.

What exactly should she wear to a casual bar on a Friday night in hopes of possibly running into her boss she didn't want to *want* to date?

Chapter Eight

B lake stopped listening to Keith as soon as the glass shattered by the bar area. His gaze zeroed in on the back of a pair of long and lean legs leading to a sexy ass, narrow waist, and cascade of dark wavy hair. She balanced on insanely high heels and giggled as she danced back away from the fallen drink. The bartender flushed and sputtered an apology, but Blake barely registered anything but the way his body tightened with desire.

He looked at his brother and saw an amused smirk in place. With more bark than intended, he snapped, "What?"

"Nothing."

"It's not nothing." What the hell had they been discussing? Something about Keith's latest personal property investment. He liked to keep on the pulse of the market.

"I'm impressed."

"About what? The way I closed the med center deal or wrangled the changes in the mall contract?" Although the way his brother's gaze never left Kira, perused her a little too slowly, he knew exactly what the man was talking about. And didn't like it one bit.

Keith shot him an uncharacteristic grin. "Your secretary. She's managed to impress me."

He conjured the image of Kira waving goodbye to him earlier that evening and telling him she hoped he had a nice weekend. "Her *intelligence* impresses me, too," he said as a reminder to both of them that her competence was what they needed to focus on—and not her other...assets. He whipped his head back to observe the brunette with the long legs. That giggle. So unique as it danced through the autumn air, into their booth. And into his brain. So much for ignoring her other enchantments.

"And I'm pretty sure she's sitting at the bar with Tish."

"So she is." He had to work to keep his response nonchalant. Funny how he could recognize her from across a crowded restaurant. He glanced at his watch. He needed to get out of there before he approached Kira and— "It's late. I have to get back to the office."

Keith choked on his whiskey. "It's eight. Besides, I think Tish just spotted me. It would be rude to leave without saying hi." He slid some bills in the bill plate, and the two men approached the bar. Blake listened again for her signature laugh. Even with her hair down and her back to him, his body still reacted. How did she draw him in without even trying?

Tish's eyes widened. "What are you two doing here?"

Blake laughed at her surprise. "Getting a drink, like you, I suppose." He glanced past her to Kira. "Ladies." His brother sidled up to her side of the bar. "Hey."

Tish picked up her martini glass and slid off the stool. "I see another friend of mine. Keith, want to meet a model?" Then, with her glass raised above the crowd, they snaked their way to the opposite side of the U-shaped bar.

Kira wiggled into the abandoned seat and crossed her legs, her skirt hitching to mid-thigh. "What kind of drink?"

"Excuse me?" It was difficult to remember he didn't mix business with pleasure when she crossed her legs like that. If he touched her skin, would it be as soft and smooth as he imagined?

Her big brown eyes blinked at him with innocent inquiry. "You said you were here for a drink, which makes sense, since it's a bar, but what do you drink? Anything *fun*?" She said fun like she was challenging him, and he agreed. "I suppose Scotch wouldn't be considered fun."

She shot the bartender a disgusted look. Dramatically rolled her eyes and refocused on him. "Oh, ugh. Borrrrinnnggg."

He snorted, hating how much he enjoyed her teasing. He guessed he deserved it, so instead of acting all offended, he laughed and countered, "There's nothing wrong with traditional."

She gripped his arm—his bicep—and electric shocks coursed over his shoulder and tightened in his cheek. "Scotch is like for eighty-year-old men. Not some thirty-year-old CEO."

Stepping closer, inhaling her tropical scent, he lowered his voice, "How do you know how old I am?" She leaned forward, treating him to a magnificent view of her pink lace bra just beneath the deep *V* of her top. "Hello Google? Really, I asked Tish."

He straightened. "Funny."

She lifted her glass to her lips. "What is?"

He shouldn't admit it. He should keep his mouth shut. But he wanted to see her reaction, and he hoped it would open up the conversation for further discussion. "I thought about doing the same thing."

She curved her lips upward in an enticing smirk. "You thought about asking Tish how old you were?"

He laughed. Witty and gorgeous. "About you." Too much more time with her and he'd be tempted to take her home.

Hell, he was already tempted. Had been tempted since the first day, really. Something in the way she'd reprimanded him over three espresso shots stuck in his mind and wouldn't let go.

She took a long sip of her sticky sweet Mai Tai and gave him a closed-mouth smile. The deep *V* of her top drew his attention to her breasts, and he nearly groaned when he noticed the outline of her hardened nipples through the fabric. But it wasn't a crime to admire a beautiful woman. Just one who happened to work for him.

He shouldn't have come over here. Not at the end of a long week with Kira occupying so many of his thoughts. "So, would you like to tell me your age?"

She re-crossed her legs, drawing his attention to her smooth, bare skin. "It would be more fun if you guessed."

He shook his head. No way would he dig himself into that hole. "Guessing has never worked in my favor." She pouted. He waited. She caved. "Fine. Twenty-five."

"I would've guessed younger," he admitted.

Her nose wrinkled. "My early twenties weren't good years for me."

Interesting. "Why not?"

She held up her empty glass. "No goals. A spontaneous and very bad haircut." She smirked. "I was going through a… transition."

His gaze landed on her hair, and for the briefest moment he had the wild instinct to tuck a piece behind her ear, to use that action to cup the back of her neck and feel if the dark strands were as soft as they were shiny. "And now you're not?" The vigilant bartender took her empty and handed her a full one. She said thanks and looked at Blake over the rim as she took her first sip. "Oh, I'm still transitioning, but at least I have a job, a goal, and my hair is longer."

Her hair, loose and flowing, tempted him as much as her

bare legs. He could play this a dozen different ways. They both needed to relax. She'd banked almost as many hours as him since she started, and not once had she protested. They worked so well together. In fact, he couldn't recall ever having such a compatible secretary. But rather than risk saying what he really wanted to say, he said, "You do have a job. And long hair."

Her grimace betrayed her confusion. "Was that almost a compliment?"

"I—" He paused. She looked so young and fresh and eager. It was too easy to forget that he never dated employees. "Do you like working at Whitman-Madison?"

She cocked her head to the side and as if reading his imaginings from moments before, tucked her hair behind her ear. "I'm adjusting to office life. How's Brutus?"

"I returned him to the vet. They found his owner."

She leaned forward and placed her hand on his forearm. With a smile that drew his attention to her mouth and all the ways he'd like to taste her, she said, "I'm so glad he's going home."

Home. He wondered what her place looked like. He shouldn't care, but he was curious.

Tish and Keith returned, and Blake tossed back the rest of his drink and settled both their tabs.

"Thanks for the drink."

"Anytime."

Tish interjected, "Really? Anytime for a drink? Because we might take you up on that."

Drinks again with Kira? Bad idea. If he needed further proof just how terrible an idea it was, he got it when she slid off the stool, landing so close to him he could feel her heat.

She gripped his bicep. "Don't worry. We won't hold you to that. Unless you want us to."

Hell yeah, how he did. He wanted her to hold him to all

sorts of things.

Kira gripped Tish's hand and dragged her out the back door of the restaurant. "No. No, no, no. This is so wrong. I can't have a crush on my boss. I can't."

Her roommate collapsed in the car. "You want my advice?"

Kira started the engine and backed out of the lot. "Only if you're going to talk me off the ledge."

"Nope. I'm going to tell you to jump."

Every fiber in her body wanted to run back inside and drag Blake home with her. He'd helped her reach so many goals, and not just because of the money. Unlike when she'd been working for her dad, working with Blake allowed her to continue fostering. She didn't even mind the long hours, because now she had more funds to contribute toward the community. Maybe parts of the job weren't exciting, but she'd enjoyed going over the contracts and offering teasing hints that there was more to her than she'd admitted. She'd have to pick up a few more packages of pink sticky notes… But that was exactly why she didn't want to ruin things. She needed to remember who she was and why she was working for him in the first place.

"Ever since I met you, you've been focused on finding out what direction to take your career, and now that you have a chance to just have fun and enjoy a great guy, you're hesitating. Get him out of your system."

It wasn't that easy; it wasn't like she could just go up to Blake and be all like, Okay, please give me some of your magic. She snorted.

When a popular song came on the radio, Kira upped the volume. "We both know what happens to the employees who get too close. And even if he'd have me, I don't want to be a drunken Friday one-night stand."

"Ooooh. You're so right." Tish hummed along for a couple beats and then said, "We don't need men."

"You're focused on your career. That's admirable. You'll find someone when you least expect it."

Finding Blake had definitely been unexpected, and she bet her favorite sundress that no one like him existed.

Tish slouched low in the bucket seat. "Guys don't like me."

"You're perfect just the way you are."

Her friend climbed out after they'd parked and followed the path to their front entrance. "Easy for you to say. I bet you two end up having fabulous office sex."

She envisioned Blake sprawling her over his desk. "Yum." Then she frowned. "No. Bad image. Stop it. He's my boss, and we both know what happens to secretaries who want more."

Tish collapsed on the sofa and closed her eyes. "Ask Keith about a job in the legal department. Then Blake wouldn't be your boss…"

"What? No. This job isn't a stepping stone. I promised one year in exchange for a seat at the table when the new architectural plans arrive. This year will help me narrow down an organization I can really focus my efforts on." She wanted to be part of so much, but with limited funds and not enough time, she knew better than to overextend herself.

Tish nodded. "I think your interest in the community is fantastic."

That was how Kira felt and now that she'd made the leap, she could feel the excitement at being a part of the revitalization for an area that meant so much to her. "Once you start working, you're pretty much working for the rest of your life. I just want to make it mean something."

"I never knew you felt that way."

She shrugged. "You just thought I wanted the big paycheck that came with the dual degree?"

Tish giggled. "It's nice being able to buy designer."

"I know, but it's also nice knowing that because of me, our downtown might be revitalized as something to preserve history that also attracts tourists."

It took her a quarter of a century to find her purpose. No way would she let the broad chest and bedroom eyes of her boss stop her now.

Chapter Nine

"Blake?" Kira stopped in the frame of his office. After their flirting in the bar Friday night, she'd thought about him all weekend and was relieved things hadn't seemed awkward when she'd arrived that morning.

He looked up, his honey-colored eyes crinkling slightly at the corners in a friendly smile. "What's up?"

It still threw her slightly off guard how casual he acted around her, and again she reminded herself that just because the CEO was nice didn't mean he wouldn't fire her if she tried to cross the line. The problem was her inability to read him, because every time he charmed her with that knee-weakening smile, she wondered how the attraction could only be one way.

Pointing over her shoulder, she asked, "Would you please come help?"

He shoved out of his chair and followed her to the main reception area where some other staff decorated for Halloween.

"Ah. This time of year again. Need me to pin something to the ceiling?"

"I need you to lie down." She bit her lower lip, hoping he wouldn't balk at the idea. In his crisp shirt and tie, he looked amazingly powerful. What she wouldn't give for an excuse to fall on top of him again. Last time had been quick and awkward, but this time…just thinking about him prone on the floor gave her all kinds of indecent thoughts. How she could take her time enjoying the full length of his firm muscles…

One of his dark brows arched. "Excuse me?"

She swallowed her wicked ideas. "Just please lie there." She pointed to the hardwood floor. "I Swiffered, so you shouldn't get too dirty."

"Why do you want me to lie here?" he asked, even as he squatted.

She took a moment to appreciate the way his pants tightened across his ass as he crouched. He really was a specimen of a man, and it seemed almost a shame that she'd started this platonic thing when she might not have the willpower to follow through with it. Maybe when her contract ended, she could—what? She shook that thought from her head and answered his question. "It's almost Halloween."

Sitting now, he tilted back his head to look up at her with an adorable grin curving his mouth. "That explains nothing."

She smoothed her hands down her skirt, and when his gaze followed her hands to her legs and then his golden pupils seemed to darken, her stomach fluttered. With a light laugh, she said, "We need a body to outline."

He reclined and clasped his hands over his stomach, crossing his legs at the ankles. "You know, Halloween was one of my grandmother's favorite times to visit the office. I think that's why my grandfather started the 'decorate and bring your children to trick-or-treat' tradition."

She grinned down at him, well aware that should he choose, he could see up her flimsy sundress. "Little kids dressed in costumes are pretty cute. May I?"

She gestured toward his hands, and he unclasped them. "Where do you want them?"

All over her body. "I'll just—" She grasped one of his wrists and lifted his arm above his head, bending it at the elbow.

He caught on to her idea and positioned the other arm in a classic angle, adjusting his feet accordingly. Then, she took the masking tape and crouched next to his face. Tearing off the first strip she'd use to outline him, she said, "Just please stay lying down."

When he closed his eyes and whispered, "Only for you…" she choked back a sigh.

She made quick work to tape around his head and hands, but when she reached his waist, she paused. Could she be brave enough to tape between his thighs? She had him right where she wanted him. On the floor, on his back, a willing victim to her…

"Marilyn?" she called to another secretary hanging cobwebs around the receptionist's desk.

When the woman glanced over, Kira wiggled the tape and pointed toward Blake. Marilyn's eyes bulged right before she burst into laughter. "No way. How in the world did you get Blake to lie on the floor?"

He opened his eyes. "I believe it's her excellent powers of persuasion."

Kira's cheeks heated. "Would you mind?" She handed the tape over.

"With pleasure." She snapped off a long strip of tape and knelt between Blake's spread legs. "You know, we've never thought about outlining a body before. Shame that Mrs. Whitman isn't here this year."

"Mrs. Whitman?" Kira hadn't given consideration to Blake's parents, but she had no idea what they had to do with the Halloween decorations.

Marilyn ripped off a long piece of tape. "Blake's grandfather would bring Mrs. Whitman to the office, and she's the one who actually started the tradition for the staff to have their kids walk around for candy during the day."

Kira watched, envy rising, as Marilyn boldly placed one end of the tape dangerously close to Blake's privates. She didn't know why she'd called Tyler's assistant to help her when she herself could have done the deed, but something about seeming too forward stopped her, and she knew the other woman—with her rock star husband and wild ways— wouldn't bat a fake eyelash at putting her hand so close to the boss's privates.

"That's so cool," she said, not knowing what else to say. "I'm sorry about your grandmother, Blake."

Marilyn scooted to the other side of Blake's thigh. "Oh, hah. His grandmother isn't dead. She's on a cruise."

Embarrassing tingles heated her cheeks. "My misunderstanding. But in a totally good way."

"Are we about done?" he asked, sitting up and twisting around to inspect the outline of his upper body.

She placed the last bit of tape by the sole of his shoe. "I think so. Thanks."

Marilyn, with her back to Blake, gave Kira a knowing wink then took a pile of paper pumpkins from another secretary and moved to another section of the lobby. "Sure thing, doll."

Her boss hopped up. "So why didn't Marilyn get Tyler to sprawl on the floor?"

Kira shrugged. "It was my idea. He might be the CIO, but you're the CEO."

"Brilliant."

"All part of my charm."

"**D**amn it!"

Blake heard Kira swearing under her breath, and he grinned. He shouldn't find her anger amusing, but she was so cute when she was flustered.

"Need help?" he called, capping his pen and marking the page in the report with her pink sticky note.

"No, thanks. I've got it covered."

He rolled out of his chair and moved to the doorway, a mistake made clear the moment he caught sight of her. On her hands and knees, head buried under her desk, he couldn't quite figure what she was trying to accomplish, but he couldn't tear his gaze from the flimsy material draped over her ass. If he tilted his head slightly to the left, he could just make out — What an ass he was. Damn. Did he really just sneak a peek at his secretary's pink panties? What the hell was the matter with him? He swallowed. Then choked.

The noise must have alerted her to his presence, because she swung around quickly and gaped at him in wide-eyed shock. "Blake! I said I was handling it."

"Handling what?" Prickly awareness tingled up his neck. Damn, he was too aware of her, and he was pretty sure it was more than the fact that on that first day she'd said she was off limits to him. He'd asked if she was sexually attracted to him, and she'd said absolutely not. Back then he'd liked that answer. But now? Still, wanting her because she didn't want him? It couldn't be that base a reason, could it? Just because she said no to him before he'd even asked, suddenly he found himself intrigued by the challenge?

A faint red flushed from the *V* in her blouse to the curve of her cheeks. "I'm trying to straighten out the cords under there. I'm tired of the mess, so I'm clipping them and color banding them."

It was definitely more than her looks. She had a way about her that screamed tidiness, and she had a competency he enjoyed challenging. As he'd promised Keith, he'd made it a point to not keep her past six or seven on too many evenings, and surprisingly, he hadn't needed to. She kept him organized during the day and, with folders clearly labeling evening issues to tackle, he'd gained a bit of spare time as well.

"Kira, you're doing a remarkable job." Almost too good, if he compared her with his other secretaries. He'd never met a woman as efficient or as sexy as Kira. She checked every box on his requirements list for a competent employee and then some, proving that he hadn't known what he'd needed until he'd found her. His gaze fell to her stack of sticky notes. Pink and shaped like a flower, she'd used them to point out key discrepancies in more than one contract. Her enthusiasm for keeping him on track, for going above and beyond any secretary who'd ever worked for him, drove him to want to please her. Show her he was as sincere in wanting to help her as she was in helping him. He made a mental note to sweeten the pot with the other board members, so the vote for the downtown redevelopment went the way she wanted. He owed her that…and more.

Why she'd settled on being a dog walker, instead of working for a high-powered exec long before now, he had no idea. It seemed strange, but maybe she never felt she was cut out for a 9-to-5 existence. Or she'd never found a boss willing to keep her foster dogs in his office.

Her body stiffened and he heard her quick intake of breath. Then, she snapped a tie around two cords and shot him a confident grin. "Thank you. I'll admit that I like it here a lot more than I thought I would."

Considering he'd forced her hand at taking the job, he liked her answer. "Really?"

He found her sheepish grin adorable. "Well, maybe not the job itself, but some of your projects are remarkable, and I'm excited to see the dog park's progress. Plus, I saw another email about the new architectural plans for making downtown historic rather than modern."

And just like that, she'd reminded him how she was just like every other woman he'd expressed an interest in. He might feel an undeniable chemistry toward her, but even if he were tempted to break his own rules about dating in the work place, he'd never know if she said yes because she needed to stay on his good side to save her mom's building.

Or if there was something else she wanted. He'd have to keep an eye on her. Maybe going above and beyond wasn't merely to help him out, but because she was looking for something else. She *did* have access to a great deal of company information.

Focusing on work, he said, "Listen, I'm sorry to ask you on such short notice, but we have a conference call scheduled for seven tonight. Can you stay late?"

"Of course. But I need to let Tish know."

"Actually, she's our accounting part of the conference call. We'll be discussing private real estate equity investment strategies, and I'm hoping you'll be able to run the recordings."

"Not a problem. I don't mind working after hours."

She might not mind it, but he'd begun to think of her as more than an employee, and he'd been trying to keep his distance; the more hours they spent together, the harder that was. Not that it mattered when he couldn't get her out of his head, but—

Keith marched straight by her desk, grabbing him by the arm. "We have a situation."

His brother always had a situation. He thrived on confrontation, as evidenced by the gleam in his eye and the excited way he charged toward Blake's office. Once inside, he sighed with aggravation. "What now?"

Keith whirled around and rubbed his hands together. "Morris Clinic is being sued."

Damn. A hundred different scenarios flew through his brain, all with equally compelling profit margins. "The whole clinic? Not just one doctor?"

"The whole damn clinic. Discrimination."

"That's wild."

"That's luck. Good business for us, bad for their reputation. Look, we're going to need to put some pressure somewhere to get moving on finishing the medical center on Palm Street. Can't wait until the New Year."

"I agree."

Keith shot a purposeful glare toward the door. "One other thing."

Blake stared at his brother and tried to follow the conversation, but the image of Kira on the floor under the desk still flooded his mind. "Yeah?"

"Did you see the email regarding the new plans for downtown?"

Blake whipped his gaze to Kira, but whether she'd heard Keith or not, he couldn't tell. Lowering his voice and dragging his brother deeper into his office, he said, "I did."

"I have an urgent voicemail to return a call to the chairman of our board."

The chairman had been a strong supporter for the modernized downtown design, but he was only one vote. "I have voting members my side. Let me make some calls. We promised Kira—"

"No. Not *we*. *You*. You made a promise you might not be able to keep. I'm just giving you a little head's up, in case things don't go your way. She's a smart girl. I'm sure she understands how board decisions work."

"No need to upset her before the vote. I have a plan."

"Why don't you offer her some of the company's charitable funds? Let her work with our corporate gifts department a little bit more. That might soften the blow."

Placate her with something different? He'd rather stick to his word. "It won't. Besides, she already saw the email about the new historical plans from architectural."

Keith shot him that disappointed glare he'd perfected. "Fine. Play it your way. I just hope you don't lose her. She's just what you need."

Blake couldn't agree more.

Kira turned her back to the bar and pouted. "He's not coming."

Tish wiggled her empty glass at the bartender. "He might."

"He's not coming." She scanned the roped off area of The Vault, the bar the Whitman-Madison executives had rented for the Halloween party. Loud music, lots of bare skin, and no sign of her hot boss.

Her friend rolled her eyes. "Sweetie, he has to show up. This is a tradition started by Blake's grandfather, and for Blake not to show up would be—unholy toward his grandparents."

"Unholy?"

"According to legend, Blake's grandfather invented the work hard-play harder mantra. His grandmother loved a good party, and his grandfather loved to throw her one."

Even through the roaring pulse of the music, Kira heard the disbelief in her voice. "Play harder?" Seemed so contradictory to what she witnessed with Blake and his brother. "If he planned to show up, he'd already be here. And even if he does show up, who's to say he'd take the time to say hi to me? He's the CEO, and I'm just the secretary." It was almost time for last rounds, and she was tired from fending off offers from other guys. She didn't need to sit around a bar hoping to catch a glimpse of her boss.

"I can't even believe you would say that." Her friend

stepped away from the bar, swayed, and leaned back against the stool. "I'm going to ask Keith why Blake isn't here."

Kira grabbed Tish's arm to steady her. "No. Please don't." She would not stalk her boss. If he didn't want to show up, then fine. Let him not show up. Better for her anyway. "Let's dance." She'd had one too many, but she didn't want to go home with this sense of crushing disappointment hitting her full force. Since when did she let a guy dictate her mood? She didn't need to chase guys, and she was the one who kept saying she didn't want to sleep with her boss.

"He's here."

Without warning, Kira's whole body warmed. He'd asked her to leave him a list of possible costumes, and she'd offered to rent one for him, but he'd said he'd take care of it. Which costume from her carefully crafted list had he chosen? Would he go traditional in a toga or be more adventurous as Captain America? She checked her cell. Two-thirty a.m. She was surprised he'd bothered to show up at all. She glanced in the same direction as Tish but only caught the top of his head. From this distance and her vantage point, she couldn't make out his costume.

Annoyed with the way her heart sped up at the stupid thought that he was right there, she said, "I'm going to freshen up."

Her friend nodded over the bass. "I'll save your spot."

As she weaved through the crowd toward the back of the bar, Kira's gaze trailed over all the revealing costumes; her Lois Lane button down blouse and pencil skirt seemed too conservative. She thought it would be cute if she dressed as Superman's significant other, and she'd even purposefully left Superman off the list of viable costumes for Blake to wear so they wouldn't match.

In the bathroom, she ran her hands under the cold water and silently chastised herself for the uncontrollable adrenaline flushing her cheeks and the urge to unbutton her blouse just shy of indecent.

After smoothing her bun, she left her buttons intact and exited the restroom. Tish chatted with Keith and a man in a dark suit, his back toward her. She didn't need to hear his voice to know who it was.

As soon as Blake's gaze found hers, she sucked in her breath. It didn't matter that he wasn't wearing a costume. Under the charcoal suit, he wore a crisp white shirt, and his navy tie matched the buttons on her blouse perfectly. But more captivating than any costume was the way his mouth curved in a smile that reached all the way to the corners of his dark eyes. The air whooshed from her lungs.

"Kira, nice costume. Secretary?"

Keith dipped back his long-neck. "You two are pathetic. Matching outfits."

Her face heated. "Not intentionally. And I'm not a secretary. And he's not even in a costume."

Blake's eyebrow arched. "If you're not a secretary, then you are…?"

"Lois Lane." She stumbled sideways just a bit as she tried to pivot to display her outfit.

He made a noise that sounded like half a laugh and half a choke. "Lois Lane, huh?"

"Yes." She gave a short nod and giggled. "Although if you prefer, I could be a secretary to match your costume, boss."

"We're already matching." He flipped his tie over his shoulder, and the entire room faded as his long finger slid the top button from his shirt, and then the next and the next, until the royal blue tee shirt with the red 'S' peeked through. He flashed a wicked grin. "I thought I was being clever, since Superman wasn't on your approved list."

Tish's mouth dropped open dramatically. "Oh my gawd, you're a match made in a superhero comic book."

B lake couldn't believe they'd coordinated costumes so perfectly. Just one more reminder of how compatible they were. "What do you think? Do I make a decent Superman?"

She chewed the corner of her lower lip and blinked up at him. "I think I need another drink."

A shot of adrenaline raced through him as he waved to the bartender. Oh yeah. His costume had definitely thrown her off balance, and in a good way. The bartender passed him a pink concoction, and he handed it to her.

She sipped, closed her eyes, and moaned softly. "Mmmm." When she opened her eyes, she said, "You're very late."

"I can explain." He placed a hand on her lower back and steered her away from the crowd. He wanted her alone. They moved to the far corner, but the music blared too loudly to have a decent conversation. "Outside."

Once they stepped into the night, he led her down the relatively empty street, and the music faded into the distance. They walked in silence for a block before she stopped and stared into his face. "You look different. More relaxed."

With an erection pressing against his zipper, relaxed wasn't the exact word he'd use, but she was right. He felt different. Slipping his hands in his pockets to keep from touching her face, his fingers touched something else that was hers. A flower-shaped pink sticky note. He removed it and held it up.

"You caught the landscape miscalculation on the downtown parking lot."

She grimaced. "That sounds like an accusation."

"Not at all. I'm impressed."

She rolled her eyes. "Everyone seems to be impressed with me tonight."

"Isn't that a good thing?"

"It would be, if I wanted to impress people."

He'd been annoyed at having to stay in the office so late, but with the architect's issues, he had to make certain nothing was left for chance. Now, he was pleased he'd taken the extra time to figure out the calculations.

And that was just one part of the problem. If he couldn't get the finances straightened out, he'd have one hell of a fight against the board explaining why keeping the old—even though it would cost them several million more to bring the existing buildings up to code—would be preferable to demolishing and building new.

Blake squinted at her in the dim light and tried to remember all the reasons why kissing her would be a terrible idea. Then she licked her lips, and he couldn't help himself. His hands moved on their own, cupping her face and lifting her chin. When his mouth closed over hers, he tasted her sweet drink on her lips and felt his growing desire.

If they hadn't been standing in the middle of the street, he'd have his hands all over her tight curves, but the roar of a passing motorcycle grounded him, and he stepped back, his gaze landing on the rise and fall of her chest as she caught her breath. Good. He shouldn't be the only one panting.

He cleared his throat. "I've been crunching numbers and architectural plans."

She blinked and touched a finger to her lips. "What?"

The dazed expression on her adorable face tugged at him, and before he completely lost his mind, he slipped his fingers through hers and tugged her back toward the bar, the company Halloween party, and the people who would act as chaperones.

"The reason I was so late was because of your note."

She looked down at their hands and then back to his face. "Oh."

"We're going to make the downtown revitalization work, but there are financial issues I need to address with some of the board."

She chewed on her lower lip, and now that he knew how she tasted, he wanted more. Kissing her had been a mistake. But one he wanted to repeat. He had to get her back to Tish, back to where he'd be forced to keep his hands to himself.

He released her hand as she stepped back into the bar, and just before they reached Tish, sitting at the bar, he leaned in to her ear, and whispered, "I'm sorry for—crossing the line outside."

B lake thought that tiny kiss outside was crossing the line? Before she could argue, a girl she didn't recognize from the office sidled up to them and called to him in a high-pitched voice. "What a great costume! I love Superman!"

Kira stepped back, inadvertently allowing the pixie intruder enough space to sneak into his space.

"Hi, Ginny."

Tish whispered, "So much for the private party sign and security guard."

That confirmed the woman was not an employee of Whitman-Madison, but given the late hour and the lapse by the security guy, Kira did nothing more than watch as Ginny batted her fake eyelashes and pressed her chest into Blake's arm. The girl had assets and knew how to use them, that was for sure. She bit the inside of her cheek to keep from muttering about the woman's familiarity with her boss.

"I can't even believe you're here. You have to dance with me. Dance with me? Please? For old time's sake?" She slipped her hand into his and gave a hearty tug.

He frowned but let her drag him away from the group. Even as she pasted on a bright smile, Kira hoped the disappointment wasn't clear on her face. For old time's sake?

Like they had a past. No doubt she was an ex-lover. But how ex and how far in the past? Even though she had no right to be jealous, the idea of Blake dancing with an ex stung, and she didn't like it.

Tish looked at Keith. "Is that Blake's latest?"

"Blast from his past. I vaguely remember her."

"Why is Superman not dancing with Lois Lane?" her friend asked in almost too loud a voice.

Kira wondered the exact same thing, but she didn't voice her agreement. After all, he might have kissed her, but he also admitted he thought it was a mistake. She had no claim to him. He could dance with whomever he pleased, and so could she, now that she thought about it. Keith must have read her mind, because he turned to her and said, "I could use a dance or two. I'm wicked out of practice."

She laughed. "Wicked, huh? I'll bet you spent too many summers yachting in Nantucket."

His eyes widened. "I did!"

"Come on." She laughed. "Let's dance."

Tish rolled her eyes. "Great. You two can bond over New England boarding schools. I'll save your seat."

"Join us!"

"I'd rather not."

She glanced once more at her friend before shrugging and facing Keith. "Okay."

His voice hummed close to her ear as they made their way to an open space on the dance floor. "Boarding school beauty. I should have known by the way you walk."

She snorted but refrained from commenting.

"So, beauty and brains. I have to admit you're the most competent secretary Blake's ever hired."

The compliment sounded sincere, and wouldn't her life be so much easier if Keith gave her the same goose bumps as her boss? After all, the VP wasn't insisting that he keep business separate from pleasure. "I'm flattered, thank you—" Would it still impress him to know she'd pictured Blake bending the rules with her bent over his desk on a number of different occasions?

"You're good for him." He narrowed his eyes. "Even if you're overqualified." She wasn't sure if he meant what she thought he meant, but then he burst into laughter. "Don't look so worried. I'm not going to tell him. He should've read your resume."

The air whooshed from her lungs, and she swatted at his arm. "It's not funny. He only offered me the job because I said I wouldn't sleep with him."

Keith kept laughing, the corners of his eyes crinkling in amusement. "Serves him right."

She looked over his shoulder to where Blake had his arms wrapped around another woman, and it irritated her that she couldn't control the jealousy. "Doesn't matter. He has that no dating employees rule."

"It's because of our mom."

She leaned back enough to see if he was still laughing, but his smile had flattened. "Really?"

He nodded. "Our dad had an affair with an employee, and Blake saw firsthand how much it destroyed our mom."

"But he's not married." Why would it matter if he dated anyone from the company? It wasn't like he'd be cheating. Still, in a weird way that explained why he was against workplace dating.

Keith shrugged. "That's my brother for you. Stickler for the rules. Especially his own."

That sounded like a warning, but as Blake's gaze clashed with hers, even in the dimly lit room, she couldn't help but wonder if it was also a challenge.

Chapter Ten

B lake unclenched his hands and reminded himself that he was an adult. He would not punch Keith in the face. But if his brother didn't get his hands off Kira in the next ten seconds, he was not going to make excuses for his actions. He would just act. Kira was killing him with her fitted skirt and crisp buttoned-up shirt. She had killer curves, and right then he envisioned about a dozen different office fantasies starring the two of them.

Keith might not have the same ethical dilemma when it came to dating women at work, but Blake could no longer think of a single valid reason not to pursue his hot assistant. That kiss had been a weak appetizer to what he really wanted to do to her, and as the night wore on, he couldn't reason himself out of repeating that mistake. Especially when he shoved his hands in his pocket and his fingers touched the pink sticky note he'd left there.

Decision made, he forced a smile as he approached them. "Mind if I cut in?"

His brother moved out of the way. "I'm going to say good

night to Tish and head home."

When Blake finally had Kira alone, he relaxed. She looked mildly buzzed, and with a sexy grin on her face, all he could think about was getting her back to his place. This arrangement might have started as a way for her to save her mom's building, or whatever personal crusade she'd been on, but for him, it was no longer strictly business. He'd changed.

But he wasn't sure she felt the same way. There was attraction, but mixing business and pleasure with her was weird, even though he'd thought of little else. Clearing his throat, he asked, "Want to get out of here?"

She tilted her head in that adorable way and scrunched her nose. "And cross more lines?"

He grinned at her upturned face and noticed her mouth, how perfectly soft it looked, and wanted to get her anywhere but where they were. A crowded bar with lingering coworkers was not the place to repeat their earlier kiss, and his lips on her lips suddenly occupied his entire brain. "I will if you will."

She laughed. "That's the worst pick-up line ever."

"It wasn't a line." Although, with her hair framing her upturned face and the way she leaned into him, using a pick-up line might get him exactly want he really wanted.

"So where do you want to go?"

"Anywhere you want me to take you." The fragrant scent of her blurred his senses, and she'd been invading his dreams, when he found time to sleep. He wanted her, and he couldn't wait one second longer to get to know her on a more intimate level.

"Back to the office?" She grinned up at him with the look that invited him into her world, and he so longed to dive into her joy. How did she do it? Act like nothing in the world could bring her down? He'd never met someone so...happy. And he wanted to be happy. Happy in the way her body swayed to the music. Happy in the silly smile that crinkled her dark eyes at the corners.

"Or my place."

Her lips rounded into a perfect "O." Then, she grabbed his hand and said, "I'm ready."

He laughed. He'd been ready since the first moment she said his name.

He said, "So am I."

Kira concentrated on breathing. Inhale. Exhale. Inhale. After they left the building, Blake drove her to a pretty fancy part of town. The twenty-minute ride offered plenty of opportunity for her to change her mind while she sat silently focusing on deep breaths. The light buzz she'd had at the party was long gone, and she'd only had two drinks to begin with.

Her brain kept creating images, anticipating what was to come. At a red light, she slid a glance sideways and caught him smiling at her, and feeling shy, she lowered her gaze.

He placed his hand on her thigh. "This isn't very professional."

"I'm not feeling professional right now."

His brow wrinkled when he said, "Are you comfortable? With this?"

After weeks of aching for him, she wanted something to happen between them, especially if he was initiating. Her only thought was how quickly she could get him out of that Superman T-shirt. "I'm very uncomfortable." He frowned, and she touched the side of his mouth. "This shirt is too confining." She slipped one of the buttons out of place, and smiled when his gaze lowered to her cleavage.

"I'd hate for you to be uncomfortable." He swallowed and looked back at the road. "You look really good in that Lois Lane costume."

"You'll look better out of that Superman shirt."

With the windows down and scent of the ocean, she felt alive. Free.

She blew out a breath. She was nervous. It had been too long since her last time, and she hated to admit that her last lover definitely spoiled her when it came to generosity between the sheets. She'd been sad to see him go, but he'd proven it wasn't her but her connections that mattered. At least with Blake, if he initiated things, it wasn't for any reason other than him wanting her.

He cleared his throat. "Okay. Usually this is when you say something more."

"More? Like what?" What else could she say? Her actions spoke volumes.

"Like, do you want to talk about this?"

He wanted to talk about this? The fact that she was in his car and they were clearly adults and heading somewhere to be adults. And then a light clicked on in her head and she laughed. "Okay, fine, Blake. I'll say it. I was wrong."

"Excuse me?"

She threw her hands up in the air and let them drop to her sides. "Oh my gawd. You're going to make me say it. Fine. Fine! I was wrong. I said I didn't want to sleep with you, but I do. I'm in your car. I'm dressed like Lois Lane, and you're wearing—that adorable Superman shirt. You win. You're irresistible."

"Considering that's the furthest thing from what I expected you to say, I think I'll just keep focused on the road."

"What did you think I'd say?"

"I was just wondering if you wanted to know where this is going."

"Blake, you're adorable. I know what this is, and I—well, let's just"—she shrugged—"see where this takes us?"

They passed by the gated guardhouse, and as she read

the sign, THE AMBROSE, a whole flood of memories from her childhood etched in her mind. He lived in a gated community where the residents banked over a million a year, easily. As they drove deeper into the development, she noticed the impeccable landscaping. Not one blade of grass was out of place.

Side roads led to large estate homes and some charming two-story villas. Straight ahead, under an impressive arch, a high-rise filled the horizon. Blake drove toward it, veering right and then into the garage underneath the facade.

He parked his SUV in a spot with a RESERVED sign and placed his hand on her thigh. "Wait here."

While her skin flamed where he'd touched her, he hopped out and strode around the back. Kira almost disobeyed, but she found a certain charm in Blake's chivalry. When he opened the door, she swiveled sideways and looked into his face as her skirt rose dangerously up her leg.

As she'd hoped, his eyes widened slightly. Just enough to give her the confidence to confirm he was interested and this was leading exactly where she hoped it would lead. This flirtation was all so silly, really, when they were both adults and both wanted the same thing. A few hours of blissful physical enjoyment.

He slipped his hand in hers. "Come on."

She glanced around purposefully. "I'm impressed."

"With the parking garage?"

"That you brought me here." Why a gated community with mansions and high-rise condominiums and lakes with fountains and a golf course? She'd assumed he lived in a townhouse by the beach or somewhere closer to the buzz of downtown. Who was he really?

"Where else would I bring you?" He slipped her hand through the crook of his arm and led her toward the elevator. It all felt so charming, like they were returning home after a date, when they hadn't ever really had one, and she swallowed her hesitation. She didn't want to think about possibilities. They were temporary, and she was one in a long line of women to hold his arm. But as they entered the elevator, and he slipped his key into the space marked "Penthouse" she couldn't help but fear the feelings bubbling inside her. Perhaps going home with him had been a bad idea. "I don't know. I did suggest the office. Maybe a hotel."

His fierce gaze pinned her in place, and when he spoke, shivers danced along her body. "This isn't a hotel kind of encounter."

"Oh." She paused. He surprised her with his sentiment. Did he really mean it? How many other women had he impressed by bringing them to his fancy penthouse? To lighten her serious thoughts, she teased, "But you didn't rule out the office."

"No. I didn't." He tugged on her wrist. She leaned into him and had just enough time to catch the intention in his eyes before his mouth descended upon hers.

Warm, soft, and powerful, his lips shot tingles down to the depths of her stomach, and this, this uncontrollable surge of longing, hit her right there. He kissed her as he backed her up against the wall. The way his mouth moved over hers had her forgetting how she'd been so sure she wouldn't want to sleep with him. He gripped the back of her neck, tangling his fingers in her hair, and she inhaled his delicious, seductive scent. When his tongue swept over her lips, she heard him groan. She let her hands roam, up his arms, over his broad shoulders, and across the wide expanse of his chest, over the smooth fabric preventing her from touching his skin.

The weight of him held her captive, and when he stretched her arms above her head and clasped them in one of his large palms, she arched into his chest.

Everything came into focus. The whole reason she'd been

at loose ends stemmed from not having direction. With Blake, she finally had a goal. He had no idea what he did for her self-esteem or the wild thoughts in her head, but ever since she'd knocked into him and decided to fight for something—her mom's vision for the community—she finally felt like she was making progress. She could do this.

She kissed him back with all the desire and longing she'd held inside over the past two months, but with her hands pinned above her head, she couldn't touch him the way she wanted. She needed to feel his body, rub her hands over his skin, but he held her firmly in place, and when his free hand ran up her stomach to cup her breast, she moaned.

The elevator doors dinged open, but instead of releasing her, he wrapped an arm around her back and lifted her into him, carrying her to his door without breaking contact.

Kira had never really thought about those scenes in the movies when the couples made out on elevators and fell through the doors still tangled together, but now, with Blake's powerful gait taking them into his foyer, she shivered from the anticipation and the sheer desire of him as he deepened their kiss. He kicked shut the door and then set her on a table or a ledge of something in the foyer, and with one swift motion, lifted the button-up blouse over her head, slid the straps over her shoulders, unclipped her black strapless bra, and exposed her breasts.

She laughed. "That was efficient."

"You did say that shirt was uncomfortable." He licked his lips and then cupped her breast, brushing his thumb over the nipple, pouring liquid fire through her entire body.

She resisted the urge to cover herself with her hands and instead reached for his shirt. She grabbed and tugged, but the buttons held firm. Her fingers pinched them through the holes and mercilessly yanked the fabric apart. A faint smile hit her lips at the sight of the Superman T-shirt, but he wasted no time dragging it over his head. When she could finally touch his exposed chest, she ran her fingers over the fine hair scattered over the hard planes of the muscles. He was built for power, and she clutched on to his biceps, felt the muscles between her own thighs clench, and gave a triumphant laugh at the way just touching him could elicit such a physical reaction from her.

Without a care for what her words meant, she said, "I have been aching to do this since I landed on you."

He grabbed her by the arms, lowered his head to her neck, and licked. "Delicious."

As his mouth trailed hot kisses over her collarbone to the tip of her nipple, she lost her grip on everything but the way he made her feel. "Oh yes."

He ran his hand up her thigh, lifting her skirt. His fingers hooked over her panties, and with one tug, they slid down her legs.

Through the haze of desire, she sank against him while his hands explored her exposed skin. She wanted this man desperately. His energy, his commanding power. And she wanted his hands on all her sensitive parts. His touch ignited fires over every inch of her skin, and she wanted the feeling to go on and on.

The heat tingled over her chest and down her stomach. Nothing else mattered but the heat of his mouth over hers and the dizzying effect his touch had on her body. Rocking into him, she undid the belt, buckle, and zipper of his pants. Using her heels to hook the sides, she shoved his pants to his ankles. He kicked out of his loafers and stepped out of the pants.

They wouldn't even make it past the foyer. She'd have him right here, and she couldn't imagine wanting anything more than to feel him pressing into her.

Until her back hit the light switch and the light flicked on. The reality of the situation flashed in front of her eyes, and the conversation in the car hit her squarely in the chest. It wasn't just about seeing where this went tonight. It would be about how they faced each other in the office on Monday.

She blinked and slid off the side table. "Blake."

He released her, and she heard him sigh. "I've lost you."

Amid the relaxed Key West décor, beachy and definitely so completely opposite his uptight work persona, she recalled the real reason why Blake even knew she existed. The building. The contract. How many secretaries had hoped to be in her exact location, and how many had he fired for such advances? She might be having fun with the temporary gig, but if she forgot for one moment what usually happened to women who overstepped their place in the office…

Kira wanted to express the thoughts flooding her mind, but she couldn't clarify them. How was she supposed to ask if he intended to let her go like he had the others? She didn't figure that he'd bring her here, sleep with her, and then renege on their deal, but… "Your rule." She whispered the final words like they were dirty and waited until comprehension lit his honeyed gaze.

A strange warmth flooded her as he wrapped her in his arms. "What rule?"

"You're against workplace dating."

He cursed under his breath. She'd been staring at the floor, and then he was in front of her, his thumb brushing over her cheek. The heat from his bare chest warmed her, and as he uncrossed her arms, he said, "You know what they say about rules, right?"

She saw the desire in his eyes and hoped he meant something about breaking them. When he opened the side table's drawer and pulled out a pad of sticky notes, she asked, "What are you doing?"

"Rules are meant to be broken, and I'm looking for a pen so I can write down on paper how certain I am I want to break them." He continued to shove around items in the drawer.

"I have one in my purse." She unsnapped her clutch and handed him a pen.

He took it and read the inscription. "The Fresh Bean. Nice."

"It's my favorite one."

"Thief."

"Rule breaker."

He scribbled something almost illegible, and she grinned when she read it. *Both parties, by signing this sticky note, do hereby agree to mix business with pleasure.*

After signing and dating the sticky, he handed her the pen. She signed it and then with a playful little smile, she slid out of her skirt, standing naked except for her heels under the chandelier. "Trick or treat."

Blake's gaze followed the fabric to the floor, and he groaned. "You're killing me."

Before she could respond, he grabbed her and anything she might have mumbled disappeared when his mouth covered hers, warm and with just enough force to cause her to forget the foyer décor.

"I'm taking you to bed. Right now." He covered one hand over her eyes. "You can look around later."

She let him steer her forward to the left, around something, and then her heels stopped clicking and she could tell this room had plush carpet. He removed his hand. She blinked. He scooped her up and spread her on the bed, and as she fell, she hoped she'd remember this was just temporary in the morning.

"Now, where were we?" He nudged open her legs and braced one hand on either side of her head.

"Yes." Kira nodded, unable to think of a single thing to say besides yes.

Blake's gaze trapped hers for a moment and then his mouth curved in a devilish smile. "Stay."

She obeyed as his tongue trailed between her breasts and over each nipple, shocks of electric pleasure sending currents rushing through her. When his tongue reached her core, she arched and gasped, her hands automatically reaching for his head. The suction on her sensitive flesh shot stars behind her eyes, and as she panted, she begged, "Take me. I need you inside me." She clutched on to him and begged. "Please. Now."

He slipped on a condom and took his time as he entered her, inch by inch. She wanted to thrust her hips to rush him, but he placed one open palm on her lower abdomen and pinned her in place. Wiggling didn't help, and he apparently decided to ignore her pleas.

With an evil grin, he said, "Don't rush this."

She growled, an aggravated sound that turned into more gasping as the tight ache climbed to an unbearable torture. "Please."

He must have sensed her desperation, because he chose exactly the right moment to increase his speed, pumping into her with long strokes and reaching between them to rub the sensitive flesh. She screamed his name, her muscles flexing wildly, until all the energy drained from her body. With the heated rush still subsiding, Blake continued to glide into her and work his fingers along her exposed skin.

The air caught in her lungs, and even having just come with so much force, the building pressure caught her off guard. Within moments, Blake tensed and his body jerked, and then a second orgasm tore through her, leaving her breathless and shocked that she'd just experienced the infamous multiple orgasm.

She collapsed against the pillows and stared at the ceiling. "That was—" She covered her face with her hand.

He slid out of her, and she wanted to protest but couldn't find the energy. Instead, she listened to the water run and her stomach rumble.

He exited the bathroom and positioned himself between her thighs, his head by her stomach. "Hungry?"

As if on cue, another grumble sounded. "Guess so."

She closed her eyes but felt the mattress move as he shifted his weight. "Stay here. I'll find us snacks."

Too curious to stay put, she hopped out of bed and followed the lighted hallway to the kitchen. He looked up, an adorable but guilty expression on his face, and as she registered his closed mouth, puffed cheeks, and hint of laughter, she glanced at the counter and saw an open sleeve of coconut macaroons.

From the beginning, Blake had managed to surprise her, acting out of character from the image she'd had of the CEO in her head, and this food-foraging Blake was no exception. She joined him at the counter and pinched a macaroon between her thumb and index finger. "These are my favorite. Just so you know."

She meant to pop the entire cookie into her mouth, but before she could, he snatched it and put half in his mouth, offering her the other half with a wicked gleam in his eyes.

She had to rise on her toes to take her treat, and when their lips collided, she closed her eyes and moaned, rocking into him. "Delicious."

He licked his lips and then kissed his way from her mouth to her neck and back to her breasts. She dug her fingers through his hair, arching into his hot mouth, and begging him to suck harder.

When his hands cupped her ass and lifted her to the counter, she squeaked and spread her legs, allowing him easy access to her already moist flesh. He wiggled his eyebrows as he told her to pass him a macaroon.

"What?" She giggled.

Without waiting for her to comply, he leaned into her, forcing her back until he stretched over her enough to slide the sleeve closer to him. "You're so sexy when you laugh like that."

"You're just plain sexy."

He took the cookie and crumbled bits on her thighs and in between her legs. The sprinkles looked like sugar crumbs, and she tried to figure out just how exactly she could pay him back with something similar. Then, his tongue lapped at her flesh, and she lost all thought and just felt. With unabashed pleasure, she spread her legs as he licked his way to her most sensitive spot, and with the granules manipulating her tender bud, she came with a fierce growl that had her bucking against him and then lying back seeing stars.

"Oh my." She flung her hand over her face and sucked in air, still processing what the heck just happened.

He tugged at her wrist and shot her an evil grin. "I'm not done."

No way could she handle any more excruciating pleasure from this man. Not while her body was still reeling from coming three times. But he'd already produced a condom from somewhere, and she perked up, eager to have him back inside her.

With renewed energy, she scooted to the edge of the counter and welcomed him into her slick folds. He stared up at her, his expression dazed. "God, you feel so hot."

She clung to his tight biceps, gripped his broad shoulders, dragged her fingers down his taut back, all the while fighting back the rushed wave of pleasure aching to explode, and when she felt him tense and then plunge into her, anchoring her to him with one firm arm around her hips, she followed him over the edge without a care as to where she'd land.

She'd thought she'd known what good sex was, but clearly she'd been playing with amateurs. Why on earth would any girl leave when the sex was that good?

And then she remembered he was the one who left them…

Chapter Eleven

Blake frowned at Kira's back as she worked at her desk on Monday. They hadn't had a chance to speak since Sunday morning when she'd woken him with a rushed excuse, a quick kiss. Something about needing to pick up Sadie the Shih Tzu from the vet, because one of the other volunteers had car trouble. He'd offered to drive her, but she'd already called a cab, and he'd mistakenly believed her when she'd told him she'd call him later.

He couldn't admit that it bothered him she hadn't called, because while sitting in his office, he'd been tempted to use work as an excuse to send her a text message. Then he'd found a significant error in the contract he'd been reviewing and all thoughts left his mind but redlining entire sections of one of his client's documents.

He'd expected some time to chat with her this morning, but he'd been thrown into an unexpected meeting with a client.

Once she placed the phone in the cradle and picked up the message slip, he approached her. "Do you want to talk about Saturday night?"

She handed him the phone message and smiled. "You're going to be late for Mrs. Ferguson and her yoga studio."

"Third floor?" He'd never known a woman less likely to want to talk about anything.

She winked and his gut tightened at her playfulness, slowing his comprehension as he processed her words. "Yes, and for the record, I'm trying desperately to keep work and play separate. I heard it's safer that way."

"And you're so into safety?"

"With you, I have to be."

That intrigued him. "Let's discuss this when I return."

"Sure thing, boss."

He clamped his mouth shut from the retort and stalked toward the elevators.

Five hours later, Blake returned and gestured for Kira to follow him into his office, stopping just inside, in order to shut the door after she entered. She faced him with a closed-mouth smile on her face, and it drove him crazy that he couldn't read her. She emitted such a simple, carefree attitude, but she sent complex signals hinting at deeper emotions. He didn't doubt she had many layers, and after Saturday, he wanted to make figuring her out a priority. As a cut and dry guy, he wanted to know why she presented such a puzzle.

He reached out and pulled her to him, caressing his hands up her waist, inhaling her floral scent, and leaning in to taste her lips. She gasped and stiffened, and as he stared down into her face, he sorted through a dozen different thoughts and admitted, "You're gorgeous."

It would be easy to let himself get distracted by her, but the pull was too much to deny. Every time she entered his radius, the tension between them demanded to be addressed, and after Saturday, after knowing what hid beneath her cute sundresses and closed-mouth smiles, he wanted more. But the wary look she shot him warned him he had to take a different route than a bulldozer.

As soon as he released her, she shuddered an audible breath and retreated to the corner, where the latest foster puppy slept on a plush cushion. After her quick departure Sunday morning, he'd expected Sadie the Shih Tzu, but she'd shown up with a Pomeranian, Duchess. Duchess came from a puppy mill. Animal Services had rescued her and her three brothers.

After she leaned over and checked the water bowl, she took the armchair opposite his desk. Instead of sitting in his executive leather chair, he took the seat next to her. Her look of surprise was enough to get the conversation started, and he crossed an ankle over his knee and said, "I enjoyed Saturday night."

"So did I. Thank you."

"You're thanking me for Saturday night?"

"For everything." Her gaze dropped from his. "For not being weird about this. For helping me with the building. For letting me keep the puppies here."

"I love that I get to be more involved because of you. I've always loved dogs, but I'm not around enough to own one. Fostering is the perfect compromise." He wasn't ready to discuss her building, though. During the meeting he'd received a text message that the new plans for downtown had arrived, but he still hadn't heard back from two of the board members who usually took his side. He didn't want to get her hopes up until he was certain he had the vote in his favor. He'd hate to disappoint her because he wanted so much to please her. To see her smile and celebrate with her after he broke the news that the board had swung in his favor. *Their* favor. He wasn't sure when her happiness had become so important to him, but it had.

Her face immediately brightened. "Really?"

Damn, if it was that easy to make her happy, he hit the lottery with her. "Really."

She sucked in her lower lip. "I'm not sure how to handle crossing the line. I've never done this before…"

He found her admission sexy as hell. "Neither have I." He didn't know what he was trying to tell her, so he plowed forward.

"I'm sorry if I made it awkward by coming on to you just now."

She retracted her knee from his and sat up straight. "Not at all. I was just…surprised."

He placed his palm on her thigh. "It's hard to keep my hands off you, but I don't want to make you uncomfortable."

She giggled. "Last time I was uncomfortable, I was wearing that tailored Lois Lane shirt and had to take it off."

"You did mention something about office sex."

That comment had her smiling.

She chewed on her lower lip and then said, "We should seal this with a kiss and maybe another sticky note."

He laughed out loud. "I agree."

She sank to her knees in front of him, and he automatically spread his thighs to allow her closer proximity. She leaned into him and offered her upturned face, her lips relaxed, slightly parted, and tempting him in the worst way possible. He slid his arms around her slim waist and tugged until she fell into him with the cutest little huff. When she wrinkled her nose, he kissed the tip of it, and then he moved lower to her mouth.

She tasted like coconut, and a memory hit him hard of how they'd snacked on coconut macaroons after their first round of sex—so explosive he'd lost his breath. How had they created a memory so soon? After just one encounter.

With Blake's chair lowered all the way, Kira found the perfect height to lean on his chest and kiss him. The weight of his arms around her back pinned her in place, and when his palms flattened on her ass, she sighed into his mouth. "If you need me to stay late tonight, I can order in pizza." She ran her palms over his biceps and wondered if office sex could be a possibility.

He tapped a finger to his lips. "You and I working late together. Alone. Could be interesting."

She shook her head. "We're both adults. We've stayed late before."

When he cupped her face between his hands, she let him, helpless to do anything but appreciate the delicious feeling of his warm palms on her skin. Leaning into him, she let a small hum escape.

His lips pressed against hers, and she forgot all her insecurities. When he pulled away, he said, "I want to make sure you're okay with this."

"I'm fine." Maybe he'd kept work and pleasure separate because he didn't want to cross a line, but now that they'd smudged that line, she didn't want him to have any regrets either. "But just to clarify, we're not—" How did she ask something she didn't want answered? Perhaps ambiguity would be her friend. He raised a brow. She swallowed. "We're keeping this quiet, right?"

"If that's what you want."

"I think so." She winked at him. "Want to see if I prefer to keep it quiet on this desk?"

He growled at her and stood, lifting her by her hips and placing her on the edge of the desk. "Don't move."

He strode over to the door, flicked the lock, and then positioned himself between her thighs. "Quiet, right?"

"Complete silence." She wrapped her arms around his neck and kissed him.

The ringing phone startled them apart, and she slipped off the desk to skip around to the other side.

"Blake Whitman's office."

After listening to a woman rant for a minute, he moved to stand by the phone. His proximity distracted Kira again, but as she inhaled his tantalizing aroma, she finally placed the caller. His sister, the councilwoman. She mouthed the name to Blake, and he gestured for her that he was available.

"Councilwoman, Mr. Whitman just walked into the office. May I put you on hold and then have him pick up the line?"

"Please."

After punching the hold button, she left Blake to his sister with a small wave. She returned to her desk and opened her email. Blake's door was still shut, and she could hear the deep baritone of his voice resonating through the wall. Whatever was being discussed sure sounded heated, and she didn't envy her boss his stress levels.

But she had her own issues to worry about, like how to handle the fact that she was now another notch in Blake's bedpost.

"B lake?"

He glanced up and waved Kira to enter. He pointed to the Bluetooth in his ear and nodded as if the caller could see his gesture of agreement. "Yes, yes, that's fine, Krystal. Thank you."

He tapped the earpiece and stood. "Guess what?"

Her face lit with a smile, as if sensing his excitement. "What?"

"Krystal found a home for Duchess. After only an hour

on the website."

He watched her smile fade and her gaze shift to the gated area in the far corner. "Oh." She nodded. "That's good." Her ponytail swayed as she walked over to the Pomeranian and picked her up. "Isn't that good, Duchess?"

Something bothered her. The whole point of fosters and the rescue was to land the dogs in permanent homes, so finding out that Duchess was going to be adopted should have excited Kira.

"What's wrong?"

She turned her face away from him. "Nothing." Then, "Why did Krystal call you?"

"She said she tried your cell, but I guess she doesn't have your work number."

"Oh. Right." Still, she didn't look at him.

When he heard her sniffle, he hustled across the room. "Tell me what's wrong."

"I try not to, but I get attached to the dogs I foster." She sniffled again. "I don't know what my problem is, because I know I'm a temporary caregiver. So, really, I'm happy for them."

"Do you want me to come with you?"

"Where?"

"The rest of the message was Krystal asking if you could meet her at The Fresh Bean. She's hoping to trade you for another foster."

Now she did look at him, and he couldn't mistake the sadness flashing in her dark eyes. Without thinking, he wrapped her and the Pomeranian in a hug. "It's going to be okay."

"I'm so happy Duchess is getting a home."

If this was Kira happy, then he hoped to never see her sad. "Come on. We can walk. The office can spare us for an hour."

They packed up Duchess's supply bag and hooked her

into the leash. The small dog wagged her tail and hopped around. On the mile walk to The Fresh Bean, Blake couldn't help but notice how Kira gripped the leash and slowed her pace as they rounded the final block. She'd been silent up until that moment, but as soon as The Bromwell Building came into view, she tensed, and he heard the fake cheerfulness in her voice as she blabbed to Duchess.

"So it's going to be so great for you to get this new home. And you'll be with someone forever and ever. No need to worry at all. I'm sure your adoptive parents are going to love you and take care of you."

He hated how hesitant she seemed walking next to him. Today she'd worn her usual sundress and sweater set, but instead of stilettos she had on a pair of strappy flats, making her shorter than usual. Her features were refined and delicate, and in her sadness, he thought she looked vulnerable. He swallowed back the urge to protect her from her pain.

In just under fifteen minutes, they'd arrived at their destination. Krystal sat with one of those wrinkly dogs by her feet, and both the dog and the woman stood upon noticing them. Duchess tugged forward, forcing Kira to speed up her reluctant steps or choke the Pomeranian.

"Thank you so much for meeting me here!" Krystal hugged Kira and then looked up at Blake. "I can't tell you how thankful we are for your generosity. I'm floored by your commitment. Absolutely stunned."

He flushed under her gushing, but he smiled like a gentleman and shook her hand. "It's the least I can do, and I have Kira to thank for pointing me in the right direction. There are so many worthy causes."

She bent and stroked the top of the other dog's head. "This one's mild-mannered, aren't you, girl? You're ready to walk back to the office with Blake and me?" She looked up at Krystal. "What's her name?"

Krystal frowned. "You walked here?" To Blake she said, "I told you I could come to your office."

"It's not a problem."

"It is, but I can drive you. This is Honeybear. She's a Shar Pei with a heart condition."

"Oh no!" Kira grabbed both of Honeybear's ears and stroked them. "Bad heart, baby? Are you on medication?"

"She's on two different heart pills. I can fill you in on the ride back."

Kira chewed on her lower lip and looked at him. "Would you mind if I ran up and said hi to someone? I promise to be quick."

He nodded and turned to Krystal. "I'll help you load the car with these two. Unless you'd like to get a coffee first?"

"I'm good. Do you need one?"

"Sure." He popped into The Fresh Bean, ordered and received his two regular coffees, and met Krystal back outside. Still no sign of Kira. "Let's go load your car."

He helped her move some paraphernalia into the trunk from the backseat, and just when he almost volunteered to enter the building and retrieve Kira, she exited, tissue in hand, eyes slightly puffy, and a smile pasted on her face as she climbed in the back seat with Duchess and Honeybear.

"Sorry to keep you waiting."

It was killing Blake. Kira hadn't been gender specific when she'd said she wanted to see someone, but he had no right to ask whom she'd seen. He didn't like the uncomfortable feeling, but he wouldn't pry—it wasn't his business. Before Kira, women had come and gone; he'd never thought twice when they'd moved on.

Now, his usually controlled facade had a scratch from the unfamiliar sliver of jealousy. He was in trouble. Big. Big. Trouble.

Chapter Twelve

B lake forced himself to focus on the words on the page and not the pink toenails standing next to him at the copy machine. The rest of the week they'd been so busy and made such an effort to keep work strictly professional. No wonder he'd never mixed business with pleasure before. It was damn hard concentrating on contracts when all he wanted to do was bend Kira over his desk.

"I can handle making a few copies on my own." She shot him that grimace that revealed her exasperation whenever he did something she found bothersome. Like hovering over her after hours.

"I'm here for your own protection. It's late."

As if to protest, Honeybear scooted closer until her jowls drooped over his loafers. Kira bent and lightly stroked the dog's wrinkles. "I know, sweetie. You're here to protect me."

He snuck a peek at the back of her legs and flexed his fingers. He would not grab her ass. He would not touch her in the copy room. He was a grown man, but she'd been sending him suggestive signals all day, and he couldn't wait to get her back in his office.

His cock grew as he recalled some of the office fantasies he'd concocted since they'd willingly blurred the lines between work and play, boss and employee, and he coughed to cover up a stifled groan. "Some protection."

"Honeybear can tell when you're not being nice, and she's already feeling bad because her owners abandoned her."

The last of the pages ejected from the copier, and she neatened the stack. "All done. Time for Honeybear to get her evening walk."

The Shar Pei's open mouth and excited panting squeezed something in Blake's chest. He hated to see the dog so eager and ready because she might seize at any moment if something excited her too much.

"Easy, girl." He stroked her head. Then he grabbed the papers and said, "I'll grab her l-e-a-s-h and meet you by the elevators."

She grinned up at him. "You're an amazing man, Blake Whitman."

And just like that his heart contracted again, only this time it wasn't with sympathy for the dog. It was for the woman and what she'd done to him. She'd changed him irrevocably, as evidenced by his desire to walk a dog instead of redlining the latest investment philosophy proposal.

His face must have betrayed shock, because she immediately stuttered. "What? I didn't mean—I mean—"

"No." He shook his head and smiled at her, touching her cheek. "No, you can't take it back. You said it. You think I'm amazing."

She swatted his shoulder. "Just get the l-e-a-s-h."

He hooked a finger under her chin and gave her a quick kiss. "This better be a short walk. I have plans for when we get back to my office."

"**O**ffice sex *is* still an unfulfilled fantasy of mine." Kira licked her lips and shot him her best *want you* smile. Heaven help her, but Blake had managed to take front and center in all her daydreams, and if that wasn't bad enough, she even imagined hot office scenarios where he stripped her slowly and made her beg for him. She'd never wanted someone so — thoroughly — and even when she wasn't at the office, she wanted to be.

"Technically, this is the copy room, not an office, but if that's an offer?"

Her pulse sped up. All thoughts about anything other than Blake naked and bending her over his polished desk vanished. "It is."

His smile turned predatory. "Then let's make this a short walk. Very short. After all, Honeybear does have a heart condition."

Blake gave *her* a heart condition, and she giggled at the tension mounting in her whole body. "Shortest walk ever."

Her heart thunked. Every cell in her body ached to be skin on skin with him, and she kept having to slow her pace as they made their way back to the office. Once there, the Shar Pei ambled into her corner of the room, content to lounge on her cushion.

A wicked smile curved across her mouth as she slipped out of her sweater. "I believe you said you had plans?"

Blake's eyes widened and a low moan emanated from his throat. He crossed to the wet bar in his office, washed his hands, dried them, and then began rolling up his sleeves. "Take it all off."

Kira had never felt more desirable than she did when he looked at her. If someone told her she'd be performing a strip tease for her boss, she'd have snorted in their face. But even when she'd first fantasized about him, it had been fairly vanilla compared to the way she lost all her insecurities and slipped out of her shoes with a tiny twirl.

I want you, he mouthed, and she mouthed the words back, adding to it. *I want you to take off your clothes.*

One of his eyebrows arched, but then he unbuttoned the top couple buttons, dragged the shirt over his head, and placed it over one of the guest chairs. When he turned to face her, she licked her lips, staring at the wide expanse of his chest. Dear Lord. She moved forward, eager to feel his arms around her.

He caught her by the upper arms, and whatever she'd been about to say flew from her brain. All she could comprehend revolved around his palms sliding over her shoulders, up her neck, to cradle her hot cheeks.

Her breath hitched, and she lifted her chin and closed her eyes in anticipation of his kiss.

But she didn't anticipate a tornado, and when he literally swept her off her feet, cradled her to his chest, and planted his lips to hers, the impact devastated her central nervous system. The surge of pleasure that pushed the building need lower, between her legs, sent waves of electricity racing over her skin. She clung to his neck, his shoulders, dug her fingers through his thick hair…messed up his controlled appearance.

Her mind blanked on everything but the way his mouth moved over hers, claiming her completely. All that mattered was the fire rushing through her veins, the driving need to grab more, wiggle closer, expose herself.

He lowered her on to the edge of the desk, sliding into the *V* of her thighs, and pressing his body into hers. "You are so sexy," he said with a low growl. She giggled, and his eyes darkened. No one had ever looked at her with such intensity. "You think it's funny I want you so badly?"

Feeling light-headed and seductive and…womanly, she leaned back and ground into him. When he groaned, she smirked. "Yup."

He reached around her to slide some files to the side and then pressed on her chest until she lay flat. Bending over her, he explored her curves, from her hips to just below her breast. "How about now?" He bent and kissed just inside the spaghetti strap of her sundress. "Do you still think it's funny?"

Another giggle escaped from her mouth. She couldn't help it. She could feel the proof of his desire, and it empowered her. Made her bold. She flattened her palms on his abs and ran them up his chest. Amazing. Tight, firm, and incredibly male. She wrapped her legs around him and hooked her ankles.

She couldn't look away from his face as he pushed the straps down her shoulders. She loved the way his eyes clouded and his breathing deepened. He made her feel so incredibly sexy. When her breasts tumbled free, he used both hands to cup them.

"I." He massaged them, sliding his thumbs over her pebbled nipples.

"Want." He flicked his tongue over first one hardened tip and then the other.

"You."

Liquid fire rushed between her legs, and she didn't even try to silence the appreciative moan that escaped from deep within her throat. She'd never known her breasts to have such control over her entire body's pleasure system and wondered if she could orgasm from just his teasing licks to her nipples.

Her dress bunched around her hips, and she breathed, "This is too good to be true."

"I knew—" He grunted. "I knew it would be like this the moment I saw you."

Like a tornado, she thought. Appearing out of nowhere, unpredictable in direction, upending everything in its path.

"Too many clothes," he complained, shoving up the hem of her dress and dragging down her panties until they caught on her spread thighs. Then he lifted her legs to the ceiling, plucked the fabric from around her ankles, and smiled down at her with his face framed by her calves.

Using just one finger, he stroked the flesh. Her pulse skipped and she slid off the edge of the desk, pushing on his chest until he fell back into the chair.

When she unbuckled his belt, he reached into his pocket and pulled out his wallet, sliding out a condom and tossing the billfold on the desk. As she unbuttoned and unzipped his pants, he toed out of his loafers. Then, she sank to her knees, dragging the pants and boxers down in one motion. But before she could touch his erection, or taste it, he lifted her by the shoulders, spun her around, and bent her over the desk.

"I'm so ready for you."

She bent her right leg and placed her knee on the desk, arching and glancing at him over her shoulder. "Oh, yes, please."

After tearing open the condom wrapper, he sheathed himself. At the same time he slid into her, he wrapped a hand around her hips until he found the sensitive spot that shot her over the edge.

Chapter Thirteen

Blake scanned the day's agenda and grabbed the file he'd need for his next meeting. He read the summary Kira had attached, and something about it bothered him. She'd typed more than a dozen summaries already, and he usually eyeballed them without hesitation. This one caught him off guard.

He scanned it again, opened the file folder, and flipped through the contents. She'd marked insightful sections and placed sticky notes with key questions over dubious subsections. Her analysis of the property matched his perfectly, and he had a sneaking suspicion why the summary bothered him.

With a couple clicks, he sent an instant message to his human resources director and then he sat back and closed his eyes until he heard the telltale ding of an incoming email. If anything could have shocked him more, it wouldn't have been the document he read and reread and printed and read for a third time. How could he have missed the signs? How had he not known? Now that the evidence was in front of him, all her actions made sense.

With a casualness he didn't feel, he called, "Kira?" As expected, she entered his office with her notepad and pen. Damn he loved her efficiency. "Yes?"

He slid the resume he'd printed around so she could read it. She stepped toward his desk, and he knew the exact moment she saw it was hers. Then, she sucked in her cheeks, blew out a breath, and fidgeting with the pen. After that, she strode around the chair, sat down, and crossed one leg over the other.

"Yes?" she repeated.

"Why didn't you tell me?"

"You said I was smart the day you offered me the position."

That wasn't an answer, but he couldn't decide if he was angry or impressed. Had she been scamming him? What was her game, besides her building and her charities? Maybe she *was* like the other women he'd dated—interested in him because she wanted something. He just wished he knew what. That she had access to a large amount of sensitive information shot prickles down his spine, but other than divulging the true extent of her education, she'd always seemed aboveboard. Still, he pressed. "You know I didn't mean that kind of smart. I had no idea you had those advanced degrees."

She blinked at him and then she laughed. "Are you kidding me? My degrees don't affect my job duties here."

"But you should have told me when I offered you a job. Or even while we went over your employment contract. You worked for a year at Layton Enterprises in a high-level position."

Her gaze lowered and she sucked on her lip. "I didn't fit in there."

Now that he knew her, he could see how the consulting conglomerate wouldn't really be her style, but… "Damn it. We slept together." And he'd connected with her on a different level than any other female. She intrigued him, and he hadn't been able to figure out why she seemed so different from the other women.

But with Kira... He thought he'd plucked her out of obscurity when she'd barged into his office. Though he'd assumed she was a dog walker, she was so much more. For some reason, she was playing at secretary but had advanced skills his company could use in many other ways. And she'd never said a word. Why hadn't she been honest with him?

With her hands on her hips and her head cocked to the side, she challenged him on every level. "What's that matter?"

She was right, of course. It didn't matter that she'd been in his bed and he didn't known her education level. Still, he couldn't let it drop. "It's not right."

"What's not right? That you didn't bother to read my resume or that you slept with someone who actually has a brain?"

"Ouch." She threw him off balance. Just when he'd thought he knew what he wanted, she'd tripped him—literally with that damn dog leash—and now. For once, he wasn't interested in neat and tidy. He wanted to peel every complex layer of her to find out who the real Kira was.

"What's that mean?"

Before Kira he didn't date his secretaries, but he also hadn't dated women with advanced degrees. Mostly because women with careers had hectic schedules, just like him, and they never had enough time to get a relationship going. It had always been easier to date someone with less ambitious career goals who could meet up with him when he managed a few spare hours.

This meant she hadn't been bluffing when she'd threatened to take the issue with The Bromwell Building to the city council, although he was certain his solution to the sticky mess would work.

But he'd try harder to secure the votes. Because now that he had her, he didn't want to lose her.

She huffed and grimaced at him. "Are you for real right now?"

The volume of their voices had escalated, and suddenly he didn't know why they'd continued this conversation at all. It really didn't matter. They had a contract. They had a good thing going personally and professionally. He should have guessed she was educated. It wasn't like he hadn't seen the signs. And when the year was up she'd go back to walking dogs unless he convinced her to stay. Found a way to engage her in his company. First, he'd have to be patient and get to the bottom of what made this confusing woman tick. Besides homeless dogs and threatened buildings. Make sure she had no other motives for accepting a job in a corporate office, when she'd just admitted she didn't feel like she fit in. He sighed. "I don't want to argue with you."

"I'm not arguing."

She smiled at him, and the way her tongue swiped across her lips before her mouth widened caught him off guard. Made every other thought fly from his brain. She was so damn beautiful. He shook his head in surrender. "You're right. You're not arguing. I am. I'll stop."

"So? Back to work?" She nodded her head in the general direction of her desk.

"Probably best." He stepped into her personal space. "But first." He stood and walked around his desk to lean over her. "This is a brilliant summary."

She beamed up at him. "Thank you, boss."

He chuckled. She'd always find a witty way to keep him in line, and he kind of liked it. Cupping her face in his palms, he lowered his mouth to hers.

Chapter Fourteen

Kira exited the bathroom at Blake's condo and her world shifted. She couldn't remember a time when she'd been so happy, and with Blake, each day kept getting better and better. He lounged against the pillows, one arm flung above his head, wearing a satisfied and silly smile that caught her in the heart and squeezed.

After climbing back into bed, she crawled up over his chest, kissing her way to his lips, then traced the underside of his arm with the tip of her finger. "I never expected you to be a tattoo type guy."

He closed his eyes and smiled. "Yeah. Not exactly in a spot where I'm reminded it's there."

She inched closer to kiss the symbol, barely visible, at the apex of the bicep and tricep. "Is that your zodiac sign?" How had she not noticed that before now? It left her aching to find out what else she didn't know about him. Pressing her lips to the double waves, she made her way over the bicep and up to his shoulder, pulling back just enough to see his mouth curve into a half-smile.

He opened his eyes and lowered his arm, the tattoo disappearing from her view. "Yeah."

She lifted his arm again to trace her finger over the symbol. "You are full of surprises. Aquarius, right?"

"It is." His arms dropped over her shoulders and he tugged her onto his chest.

Snuggling into him, she nuzzled her nose in his chest. Even after sex, he smelled so fresh and dizzyingly delicious. "Hmmmm."

"What?"

"That explains so much about you." She'd had an Aquarius cheerleading captain in high school, and that girl had been a born leader with a generous heart.

"It does, does it?"

"More than you know. Do you read your horoscope?" She loved horoscopes, hope, and categories. Her zodiac gave her a sense of identity, something to connect with her feelings, but it also gave her a frame with which to work. She knew her limitations and she could push them, fight against the ingrained astrological forces defining her.

"I used to." His voice sounded wistful.

He sounded like he was recalling a memory, and with curiosity winning over jealousy, she asked, "What changed so you stopped?"

"It's a bunch of hocus pocus."

She pushed off his chest and sat sideways in the bed, looking down at him. "I read my horoscope."

"And?" He reached out and traced a line up her inner thigh, sending shivers to her feminine parts.

She licked her lips and reached out to touch his stomach. His muscles flexed, and she noticed a renewed energy to his cock. "I keep reading until I find one I like."

His hand shot out and grabbed her, dragging her back onto him. He kissed the tip of her nose, even as his hardness pressed into her stomach. "Real scientific."

"It's a horoscope. It's not supposed to be scientific."

"Then why read it?"

She crawled over him and straddled his hips. "For the feeling of hope."

His large palms massaged her ass. "What's your sign?"

She moaned and wiggled against him. "Guess."

He ran his hands up her backside and over her stomach, then cupped her breasts. "Based on your personality and my limited knowledge of the zodiac, I'd guess Leo."

The way his thumbs grazed over her nipples dampened the apex between her thighs, but she didn't want their conversation to end just yet. "What? Why would guess that?"

"Am I right?"

She'd never been so enthralled by any man in her whole life, and Blake took sexy to a whole other level. The teasing was agonizing, but it felt too good to rush. "I'm not saying until you tell me why you picked Leo."

"Besides that your birthday is listed on the employment forms?"

"There's no way you remember my birthday from the HR forms."

"So then it's back to your personality." As he said this, he lifted his head to pull one of her sensitive nipples into his hot mouth. She closed her eyes as the sensations tugged low in her, and she wondered how much longer she could discuss the zodiac with her body aching for him to take her.

On a gasp as his tongue played with her nipples, she protested, "I'm a gentle lamb, not a fierce lion."

He stared up at her with a look filled with desire. "You are a lioness."

"This isn't about me. I don't have a tattoo of my sign. You do. Which means you were really into this hocus pocus."

One of his shoulders lifted in a lazy shrug, coupled with a

half-smile. "Might have been."

That smile caught her in the gut. "Something happened that you stopped or lost interest or—oh my gawd, it was a woman! You got a tattoo for a girl, didn't you?"

"Given our current position, I'm safer not answering that."

Kira laughed. She didn't care about his past lovers. But she did care about the reason behind his tattoo. She'd always wanted her zodiac sign tattooed on her, but she'd never been brave enough. Not like Blake. He'd done what she'd been too scared to do, but the fact that he even had a tattoo of his zodiac made her feel connected to him.

He rolled into her space, and with his hands around her waist and his mouth grazing hers, he said, "I'm glad you're here."

She inhaled and gripped his shoulders as she fell back on the bed. "I want to be here."

He bent down to kiss her collarbone and her neck, and with each lick the ache between her thighs increased.

A bubble of laughter escaped her lips, and she pressed her mouth to his bicep. "You're delicious."

He chuckled and nibbled her shoulder. "I like how your breathing increases just before I lick your nipple." He dipped his head and opened his mouth, but didn't taste her just yet.

As if on cue, her chest rose and fell in rapid succession, and her breath hitched and sped up when he finally, slowly, traced the tip of his tongue around her tightened nipple.

"Blake!"

She gasped when his fingers found her sensitive core and instinct had her rocking into his hand. "Again?"

As he drew her into him, she took her time exploring his body. When he tried to increase the pace, she slowed down. "Are we in a rush?"

"You're killing me. Cruel and unusual punishment."

She used one hand to stroke him and the other to cup his balls. "Good. Now you know how I feel."

He closed his eyes but didn't try to hurry her along.

Everything about him aroused her, and she inhaled his scent and kissed the light scattering of hair covering his muscles. She couldn't remember a time when she'd enjoyed a man's body so thoroughly, and her fingers glided over his pecs and abs, his shoulders and biceps, until he growled, shooting her a hungry grin.

He pinned her beneath him, and from the way he licked his lips, this was going to be better than good. "I don't know what's worse. That I want to consume you quickly or torture you slowly."

"Both," she challenged him. "Find a way to do both." He dropped to his knees and his hands stretched up to cup her breasts and toy with her nipples at the same time his tongue flicked over the damp spot between her legs. Her hands dove into his hair, and she felt the vibration of his laughter against her core. He didn't stop, even as she arched into him and her knees buckled. Wave after wave of an intense orgasm crashed over her.

When she thought she couldn't take any more, he stood and lifted her into his arms. "You're gorgeous when you come."

Her face heated, but she refused to be shy and closed her hand over his hardened shaft, trying to memorize this exact feeling, the perfect way he made her feel, the muscles in his chest, and the playful desire she could see in his eyes.

With Blake she felt this unfamiliar need to solidify what they were, because in the background, there was always this unanswered question of her career. Would they stay together for the rest of the year? Until her contract expired? Afterward? When she hopefully settled into a career focusing on pro bono cases and maybe landed a board position for a not-for-profit?

"You're lost in your thoughts again." Blake's voice dragged her back to him, and she absently stroked him. She stopped and stared at him. "Don't stop. I don't mind. But I can tell you're somewhere else."

"No. I'm right here. I'm plotting my payback."

She sank to her knees and licked the tip of his cock. He jerked, and she gripped it more firmly then sucked the entire head into her mouth.

"God, Kira."

"Just Kira," she mumbled, using her hand and mouth to stroke him until he rocked into her one last time.

She giggled again, watching him watch her and feeling so desirable. Then she spread her legs and welcomed him into her warmth. A thrill raced through her when he entered her.

An hour later, she was on the computer while he did some work at his desk.

"Interesting." She clicked on the email's link and scrolled through it.

"What is?" Blake glanced up from his papers.

"I was just looking at your spam mail, and there's a fundraiser you should probably attend. The Fort Myers No Kill Shelter is hosting a Thanksgiving dinner." She pointed to the screen.

He rose from his chair and came to lean over her, and she made the mistake of inhaling his fresh scent. The aroma sent her thoughts whirling back to his bed, one of her new favorite places.

Abruptly, she shook her head and cleared the memories. "Should I RSVP for you?"

"Maybe you should RSVP for both of us."

She glanced over her shoulder at him. His offer was unexpected, and she didn't know if he'd said it as a question or a statement. How exactly did he mean for her to RSVP? As boss/employee or as a couple? To her knowledge, he'd never asked his secretary to attend a social event with him, so this would certainly be a first.

She blinked. Okay, so this was probably one reason why Blake never dated his staff. So far they'd kept their affair quiet, but if they attended an event together… Instead of asking what kind of "both of us" he meant, she skipped around the question. "I wasn't invited."

"You could be my plus one. When is it?"

Kira eyed him for another heartbeat and then turned back around, unsatisfied and oddly deflated, to face the computer. He hadn't actually asked her to be his date, and he hadn't clarified if they would be attending as Whitman-Madison representatives or as a couple.

"A week from Tuesday."

"Perfect. Our first date." She stiffened, and he must have sensed it, because he moved from behind her to rest on the edge of her desk facing her. "Don't you want to go?"

She chewed on her lip. He'd said it. Their first date. And now they'd be announcing they were a couple. Was that what she wanted? Was she ready to take the next step?

No matter what, attending the Fort Myers No Kill Shelter dinner would give her a chance to speak with other interested animal lovers and see how they ran things in their county. That would help her better serve the Edgewater Bay Animal Rescue.

"Okay. I'd love to go."

Blake nodded and took two steps toward his office before pivoting on his heel and returning to her desk. "I should have asked if you wanted to go with me."

"I do."

"I know, but—" He shook his head, a remorseful-looking smile tugging on his mouth. "Kira, would you like to attend this event with me as my date?"

Appreciation for his consideration warmed her, and if she thought she'd be okay with just the sex without the dating, she realized she'd been wrong. It meant a commitment to take their relationship to the next level. Going on a public date with Blake excited her, and with genuine enthusiasm, she said, "I'd love to."

Chapter Fifteen

Blake eyed Kira standing across the high top table in the VIP section for the Fort Myers No Kill Shelter Thanksgiving dinner. Her red dress cupped her curves, and he'd considered begging her to skip the event and race back to his place. But she looked too good to not show off, and she'd been shy when he'd said he wanted to pick her up for their first date.

Dressed in that dress and wearing those shoes, the sight of her teased him, and on the drive to the events center, he'd concocted wicked ways to pleasure her. She was so sexy and beautiful, and their chemistry was unlike any he'd ever experienced, but more than that, he'd come to appreciate all her other qualities, too.

The ones she'd tried to hide. He'd fixated on her looks initially, but what caught him was the sound of her laugh, the way she brought him coffee, even when he didn't ask for it, and the guilty look she shot him when she broke something in the office. The shy smile she'd give him when she nailed an assessment or anticipated his needs. And don't get him started

on when she'd claim his contracts and dissect the legalese—
that was downright hot. Kira was the whole package, and he
felt like he'd only seen a glimpse of who she really was. He
wanted to challenge her and protect her and find some way to
keep her all for himself.

More than anything, despite the difficulties he'd had
wrangling with the board over redevelopment, he was
determined to make her vision of the revitalized downtown
come true. He'd tweaked and retooled, paid for additional
assessments and plans out of his own pocket to find some way
to lower costs and persuade the dissenting members to vote
in his favor. He wouldn't let her down; he wanted her to be
proud of him.

He held up the two red complimentary drink tickets he'd
been handed at check-in. "What's your preference?"

"Whatever you're having is fine with me."

"Even if it's Scotch?" he teased, pleased when he saw
recognition in her eyes.

She grinned and in a sing-song voice said, "Bor-ing."

With his lips brushing over her ear, he whispered, "What
I lack in imagination for my liquor, I make up for in the
bedroom."

Her cheeks flushed. Good. He shouldn't be the only one
hot and bothered.

"Okay. Boring Scotch, please."

Their gazes locked, and the air slammed into his chest,
knocking the wind from his lungs. Dear God, she could slay
him with one look, and he'd be damned if she took that feeling
away from him.

Even if he'd had to readjust his plans for downtown
Edgewater Bay and her building, if that was how he'd met
Kira, he was glad it happened that way. He'd make sure the
Board voted on preserving the historic downtown rather than
the shiny, new citified plans and everything would work out

just perfectly.

Kira stared across the ballroom at Blake and watched, helpless to do anything but admire the way he moved. Powerful and with purpose, he wore his suit with the center button fastened, and the way the fabric tugged over his broad shoulders made her itch to run her hands over him. She knew what was beneath those clothes, and she appreciated every inch of his powerful frame.

Her breath hitched. Her chest constricted. She'd never wanted a man more in her life, and the more she considered where this was going, the more she loved the idea that a charity for animals was their first date.

Then, he was in front of her, handing her his drink of choice. "Have you ever even tried Scotch?"

The smirk on her mouth signaled she hadn't.

"Well, I'll bet you…" He swirled the liquid in his glass, thinking.

She provided the answer, "A foot rub?"

"A foot rub that you're really going to like this."

"Oh?"

A challenge lit his gaze, and she loved that about him. That, and his sense of purpose helped shaped her these past months. All because of Blake.

They clinked glasses, but as she raised the glass to her lips, he said, "Don't lie. I'll know if you do."

She took a sip, cringed, and said, "I'm not going to lie. When's my foot rub?"

His eyebrows arched. "Really? Just like that?"

She shrugged. "What can I say?"

"That you like it!"

"But I like a foot rub more."

That earned her a wide smile that weakened her knees. "I say we leave right now, so you can collect on the bet."

She took another tiny sip. The irrational part of her wanted to grab his hand and drag him out of there. Forget the foot rub. Focus on the sex. The really amazing, hot and sweaty sex. Maybe they could find a closet for a quickie? "I think it would be considered rude to leave before we've eaten."

He shook his head and sighed. "You're right. We need to change the subject to something to help get me through this dinner."

She decided now was as good a time as any to bring up the building. "I saw your calendar for next week. There's a meeting with the architect to review the newest plans. Any chance I can tag along?"

His eyes narrowed for a second, but then he touched her arm in a way that was meant to be consolatory. "I don't think that's appropriate. Several board members will be there, plus the other partners, but none of the other secretaries. I'm really sorry."

She understood, though hearing him decline her request still hurt her feelings. She wanted to be a part of the project from start to finish. "Can we meet when you get back and you can tell me what happened? Please?"

"Of course." He kissed her forehead.

She placed her hand over his. "I'm so excited about this. I can't tell you everything that's been running through my mind."

He wrapped an arm around her waist and looked genuinely interested when he asked, "What do you mean?"

She set down her glass and leaned on the cocktail table. "Well, I know it'll take time to refurbish the downtown, but while it's being completed, I'm going to look into establishing a heritage museum. Other cities with historic downtown areas have them. How great would it be if the museum sold bricks for people to engrave their names as supporters of the area?"

"That's a fantastic suggestion." He squeezed her hand. "You have brilliant ideas for this community."

She beamed. The compliment really meant something, and she wondered when Blake's opinion started to matter so much to her. "You're not just saying that?"

"A museum is something people will really buy into, especially if they get their name on a brick."

So excited in sharing her ideas, she didn't even cringe when she swallowed more Scotch. "So what about you? Would you pay to get your name on a brick?"

"Why not? I missed out at the veteran's hospital, so this will be my first."

For too long she'd been an innocent bystander to life and all along Blake had been doing things around town. He'd surprised her in so many ways.

If she'd thought this date would be some kind of test to their chance at a future, it had proved that they could really make this happen. He obviously didn't care if people knew they were more than boss and employee. He'd been sending signals all night to anyone within eyesight by touching her arm or kissing her temple.

For once, she knew a first date would end with sex.

Chapter Sixteen

Blake pressed open the door to his condo with one arm, standing to the side for her to enter. Kira sucked in the corner of her lip and stepped into the darkened room. Within a heartbeat, the light flicked on, and he locked the door behind them.

He snaked his arms around her waist and dragged her into him. Her warmth grounded him, and the way she sighed in his arms sounded like everything he ever wanted to hear.

Her gaze captured him, and he wanted to give her everything he had to give. He caught her in a kiss that stole his breath and fed his wanting her, and as his tongue danced along her lips and deeper into her mouth, she grabbed on to his biceps with a vise-grip. Then, she grabbed at his shirt front, bunching it in her fists.

When he dragged her closer to him, she fell into him and sighed. "Well, that was a very warm welcome."

He kissed the side of her mouth, her cheek, her forehead. "I missed you."

"It's only Sunday, and I saw you Friday at the office."

She grinned up at him, then over at his TV. "What time's the interview on the medical center and Morris Clinic trial? I can't wait to watch you on the big screen."

He stepped back. Her tone was playful, and he doubted she understood the intensity of his admission that he missed her. That they hadn't seen each other all weekend bothered him, and he'd done everything in his power to clear his evening so he could be with her. Ever since their first date at the fundraiser last week, they'd reverted to the work-mode at work and the sex-mode after hours.

He'd had half a chance of staying detached when it was just sex, purely physical attraction, but when his need for her companionship matched his need for her body, well... This was the first time he'd actually rearranged a business meeting to be alone with her. So, even if she didn't get the implications of him altering a busy schedule for her, he certainly did.

He trusted Kira. Totally. She was exactly what she portrayed—a woman with a big heart who loved dogs and wanted to donate as much of her time and energy to the community as she could. Although he'd watched her for weeks, he'd never found evidence of any ulterior motive for hiding her education from him. She wasn't attempting to steal information or ladder climb, wasn't a corporate spy from Layton Industries. Unlike the women from many of his previous relationships, Kira wanted Blake for himself. Not for what she could get from him or what he could do for her. Accepting that set him free to care about her. Deeply.

They'd connected on their date. Conversed. No more rushed evening encounters. He wanted to take her to dinner and afterward have her sleep over. He wanted a real chance for this to work, and he shook his head, astonished by what he was about to say, but he needed to prove to her the kind of man he could be. "I want to adopt Honeybear."

As if on cue, from somewhere deep in the penthouse—

the kitchen?—the Shar Pei gave a sleepy bark. He'd taken the dog for the weekend, after he heard all the cleaning she expected to do. He convinced her vacuums and cleaner wouldn't be the best environment for Honeybear.

Kira looked as if he'd punched her in the gut. "You want to keep Honeybear? Why?"

Her gaze, seductive yet vulnerable, gripped his chest. If there was such a thing as heaven and hell combined, he was there, warring between his need to drag her into his bedroom and his need to continue this conversation. He kissed the top of her forehead and tried to explain as gently but as clearly as he could. "Because I'm not fickle. I don't just care for a week or two and send her away. If I care, I care." He wondered if she understood his double meaning.

She fidgeted with her slim hands under his stare and finally said, "But Honeybear is sick. She could die at any moment."

He slipped his fingers through hers. Was that why she liked fostering? Did this beautiful, caring woman have attachment issues? He wanted to wrap his arms around her and offer her comfort, but her fear made no sense. Most families had pets. "That's life. The things we love don't come with guarantees. But that doesn't mean we should stop caring."

She squeezed his fingers and released his hand. "I care."

Honeybear ambled up next to her, and she bent to run her hand along the dog's head. But even with her dark hair falling forward, Blake saw her blink back signs of glistening tears.

He pulled her closer to him. "I know you care. I know you do."

They settled on the sofa, and Kira shh-ed him a bunch of times as the interview started. She watched as Blake inclined his head with a bashful smile in that charming way that caught her in the gut every damn time.

After discussing the need for a modernized medical facility and a quick rundown of the progress being made on Palm Street, the anchor shifted into personal questions and asked Blake what he considered his most valuable asset. The anchor had probably meant in terms of material items, but television Blake grinned at the same time in the flesh Blake wrapped an arm around Kira and kissed the top of her head.

"My time. A very wise and beautiful woman told me once that time was the one thing she'd never get more of, and that's what made her time so valuable." He looked directly into the camera, and her heart stalled. She'd said that to him in frustration when choosing which projects to champion. Not enough time to do everything she wanted to do.

"And you certainly give your time to admirable organizations." The anchor leaned in. He chuckled, and his laughter rang through the living room. Kira collapsed back against his chest and tucked her legs to the side. Did he have any idea how much sex appeal he packed in a simple laugh? All she wanted to do was undress the man, especially when she felt the hard muscles under his shirt.

Blake clasped his hands together. "I'm floored by the community's generosity in funding worthy causes, and I'm happy to take this opportunity to ask you, the viewers at home, to save the last Saturday in February for the Just Don't DUI gala. It's to raise awareness for the real cost of a DUI, and together we can help educate everyone on preventative measures to ensure fewer incidents and accidents."

"Any final comments you'd like to share with the viewers? Maybe something fun?"

He pressed his lips together in a firm line, and then he

grinned. "This might be too philosophical, but I'm feeling it today. I'm an Aquarius, and once upon a time I let a street artist in Key West henna my zodiac onto my upper bicep. I later had a permanent tattoo inked there, and it wasn't because of a girl or a dare. It was to remind me that we all have a certain energy given to us based on when we're born, but we don't have to be labeled by anything other than how we choose to label ourselves."

Kira pressed a hand to her heart. He'd said exactly what she felt about her own zodiac sign. When she'd first bumped into Blake, if someone had told her she'd have the best sex of her life with him, she probably would have believed them. But keep her foster dogs at work? Break his no-sex rule? Spend a couple hundred thousand of his hard-earned cash on charitable donations?

Connect with him on a deeper, emotional level? No way.

"Wow, that's so not"—the anchor waved a hand up and down Blake's suit—"this suited up CEO."

Blake chuckled.

"Thank you, Blake Whitman, Aquarius man, for speaking to us about your organization. Contact information is on the bottom of your screen…"

Kira stared at the fading image of Blake and wondered when she'd fallen in love with him.

Chapter Seventeen

Honeybear's pained howls woke Blake, still dressed in his work attire after collapsing from another long day out of the office. He called the emergency vet's office and as carefully and quickly as the Friday night traffic permitted, he sped the dog to the clinic.

As soon as the vet took the dog to the back, he called Kira. Her sleepy hello greeted him after the first ring.

"I'm at the vet with Honeybear."

"I'll be right there," she said, sounding more alert.

He was about to say that she didn't need to bother, but he stopped himself. He wanted her there, and he liked her automatic insistence on being part of this. "Thank you."

Twenty minutes later, she hurried through the doors wearing the most adorable tee shirt with an image of a Shar Pei, a pair of jeans, and flip-flops.

Her face was puffy—she'd been crying. She didn't hesitate as she walked right into his hug. "What happened?"

It felt so right to hold her, and he smiled remembering the Lab and the last time she'd rushed to the clinic to be with him.

"So we meet here again."

She blinked up at him. "Are you trying to be funny?"

He'd missed her, both her body and her company. She'd left work hours before he had, and right before Honeybear had woken him, he'd been dreaming about her naked in his arms. "Just thinking how far we've come since we were here with Brutus." Which was true, given how panicked he'd been when he hadn't known where to take the injured Lab.

Kira scowled. "I remember. But how is Honeybear?"

"She's going to be fine. But the vet has referred her to a larger veterinary surgical center."

Both of her hands cupped over her mouth, and her eyes blinked back tears. "What? Honeybear needs surgery?"

"The larger clinic might be better able to assess her heart function and prescribe new heart medication that won't wear down her kidneys."

Her mouth curved into a frown and then straightened, not quite making it to a smile. "So that's good, right?"

"That's good, but they're going to keep her overnight to monitor her."

"Blake, I don't want to be alone tonight."

"Of course not. You're coming home with me."

As soon as the door clicked shut, Blake snagged Kira's hand and pulled her into a tight hug. It was exactly what she needed, and she linked her fingers around the back of his neck and dragged his head closer to hers. The familiar heat rushed through her veins, and she pressed her lips to his in a fierce kiss meant to convey all the emotions she couldn't express in words.

She ran her hands over his impossibly broad shoulders and down his back, pressing her hips into him and feeling his growing erection. His breath hitched when she wrapped a leg around him, and for several heartbeats they kissed. Then, the floor disappeared from under her feet, as Blake carried her toward his bedroom and straight into the bathroom.

She leaned back enough to look in his face. "What?"

The gleam in his eye told her he had a plan. "Shower."

He placed her on the plush bathmat and turned on the water. She ripped off her clothes and stepped under the rain showerhead, closing her eyes and letting the hot water seep into her skin. When his mouth closed over hers, she let him devour her. He came at her with all the force and power of a Hummer, and she backed up until her ass hit the cool tile.

He didn't even bother using soap, and she saw his intentions once he had her in the shower. As he went down on her, he lifted one of her legs over his shoulder. From the first moment his mouth closed over her clit, she moaned and it echoed against the bathroom tile.

"That's right," he mumbled into her skin. "Let me hear how much you like this."

She groaned and rocked into him. He sucked, and she saw stars behind her closed eyes. His fingers spread her wide, allowing his tongue easy access to flick her sensitive flesh and lick her over the edge.

"I'm...oh," she panted, her muscles contracting as wave after wave of sensation flooded from her body. "Oh."

He caught her under the ass when her knees buckled. He gave her one final, forceful lick and then lifted her into his arms and carried her into the bedroom.

Wet, still reeling from the orgasm, and wanting him inside her, she watched him rip open a condom.

He grinned. She wiggled and shot him a seductive smile. "Your turn."

He leaned over her and sucked on first one nipple and then the other, sending dizzying waves of pleasure through her entire nervous system. She shivered and arched off the bed.

After taking his time to tease her breasts with his tongue, he slipped his cock inside her and grinned down into her face. "Both our turns."

With each thrust, she felt her tender nerves spark to life, and when he grunted his release, she wrapped her legs around his waist and flew over the edge with him.

A fter foraging in his kitchen for food and coming up with a bottle of wine, some crackers, and a jar of jam, they'd called for Chinese delivery and stood in Blake's kitchen drinking wine while they waited.

A hundred emotions raced through Kira's brain before she smiled with a sadness she didn't want to feel. "What if something happens to Honeybear tonight?" A million different things could go wrong.

He pulled her into a hug and gave her shoulders a squeeze. "She's strong. The vet is good. Trust the process."

She blinked back her worry, reflecting on how easy it was to trust him. "Did you just turn philosophical on me?"

"I've come to the conclusion that it's just better to trust the process."

"Since when?" Every day she spent with him made her realize why she'd never fit in anywhere else. He got her. Knew exactly what to say to calm her—or excite her in bed.

"Since you. I threw out my rules for you, and—"

She leaned forward. "And?"

He held the glass to his lips but lowered it without taking a sip. "And I was chugging along quite nicely until you attacked me with that doggy leash, barged into my office, demanded I not demolish your building, offered you a job, and now this."

He gestured between them. "I trusted the process, and now look where we are. I think it's working perfectly."

She hadn't realized how much had taken place since that fateful day. "You do?"

"Besides wanting more of you, yes, I do."

"More? What are you talking about?" They saw each other every day. She saw him more than she'd seen anyone else lately.

He chuckled, and drew her deeper into his embrace. She lifted her face to his, her gaze flitting between his eyes and lips. "I want more time, Kira. More than scheduled meetings and breaks. I want you by my side. I don't want to hide how I feel about you."

"Because you care?"

"You know I do."

She went up on her toes and kissed him gently. "I care, too." And for the first time, she honestly believed they might have a future together.

Chapter Eighteen

"Blake Whitman's office." Grabbing the message pad and a pen, Kira cradled the phone between her shoulder and ear and wondered for the millionth time why she didn't leave the headset on her head.

"Something came across my desk, and I need you to not freak out, Kira."

She dropped the pen as her intuition kicked in. "Something bad, Tish?"

"It might be best if you come here."

She clicked open Blake's calendar. He'd waved goodbye twenty minutes ago as he'd headed out to a site meeting with two analysts and the company's top project manager. He wasn't expected back for almost two hours, so she rushed to Tish's office.

She knocked and opened the door, but paused when she saw the stricken look on her friend's face.

"Why do I think I might not want to hear this?"

"Three of the six board members are still in favor of the shiny, new downtown. Looks like your boss hasn't come through on your bargain. I wonder if he's tried to change anyone's mind."

A pain gripped Kira's chest, and she inhaled sharply. "What?"

Kira sank into a chair and stared out the window. Blake had promised to save her mom's building. She'd slept with him. They'd just discussed trusting the process, and now that process might not work in her favor. She'd really believed him when he said she was different. That he wanted more.

She was delusional. He existed on a different playing field. He might keep her for short term and when he needed to release some pent-up tension, but his proposal to change their relationship from a casual affair to a commitment was as unachievable as a trip to the moon. Lying to her about the Bromwell was case in point that he couldn't be trusted.

"Show me."

Tish slid the proof across her desk, and she picked up the two pages and scanned them. The first was an email to accounting, detailing the cost analysis requirements for the two different architectural plans, including the price of the properties not already owned by Whitman-Madison. The second was from Keith to Blake confirming that every landowner located on the downtown bayside street had signed the city council's preemptory sales agreement, including her father, Dominic Layton.

Kira held the printed emails in her hands. Tangible evidence the buildings would be bought and razed.

The papers slipped from her fingers and tears blurred her vision. Her friend hugged her and patted her back and told her they'd figure out something, but it was over. Everything was over. She'd been so dumb thinking working for Blake would keep her mother's legacy safe. All along, he'd been working behind the scenes to finagle the purchase of the building anyway. Once her dad signed on the dotted line, there was no way to hold Whitman-Madison accountable to not demolish it.

"I've got to go," she murmured. "I've got to—" Why the hell hadn't she told her dad her plan? Begged him not to sign? Because she hadn't expected Blake to go through with the acquisitions. He'd promised her that he'd try to sway the board. That he'd come up with viable options to keep the Bromwell. He accepted her foster dogs in the office. He'd adopted Honeybear. He'd slept with her and said he cared. How could someone like that have made such bald faced lies?

"How can I help you?"

"This is something I have to handle on my own. Thank you. I-I appreciate you sharing this with me."

She plodded back to Blake's office and entered and closed the door. After sinking into the space where Honeybear reclined, she crossed her legs and took the Shar Pei's head in her lap. She stroked her and told her she wasn't crying and that they'd survive this latest mistake.

She'd trusted Blake. Even fallen for him. He'd tricked her into his world, given her everything she thought she wanted, and in the end, he'd done exactly as she'd originally expected.

Honeybear closed her eyes and snuggled deeper into her lap. Kira didn't know how long she stayed on Blake's floor, but eventually the tears slowed and a numbness replaced her anger.

She didn't have to go down without a fight. She could stick with her original plan. Take the matter to the city council. They still had the final say in the redevelopment plan. As her father had pointed out, after the council chose Whitman-Madison for the design team, the corporation had to approve plans to take the community redevelopment board and the city council before they could even begin.

Determined to carve out a new plan of attack, she thought back to all that she'd accomplished since working at Whitman-Madison. She'd been able to do more for the community and make monthly contributions to her favorite charities. She didn't have to feel like she'd wasted the time she'd spent here.

Gently sliding out from under Honeybear, she stood and checked the time. Blake was due back any moment, and her face must be all blotchy from her temporary bout of hopelessness. After slipping out of his office, she made her way to the restroom and took her time calming herself.

When she returned to her desk, his head was bent over a thick binder. She tapped on the door and walked through before she lost her nerve. "Blake?"

He looked up and grinned at her. When he saw her face, his expression tempered. "Why the frown?"

Her hands were shaking, and she clasped them in front of her and tried to even out her breathing. "Is it true?"

"Is what true?"

She clenched her jaw and then said, "That half the board didn't like the new plans for the downtown revitalization?"

His mouth opened and closed. His stunned but not surprised expression told her he was aware. "You always knew that was a possibility."

That wasn't the impression he'd given her. Not when she'd shared with him her excitement over a museum and pathways. The betrayal stung. "How could I have expected you to save an entire downtown? Why would you? But I thought…" She stared at his granite face and another thought struck her. "How long have you kept it from me?"

"Don't pretend like you're so innocent."

Innocent? What had she done? She blinked and bit her lip, wracked her brain for answers. Her hands shook with anger, and tears threatened to fall. No way would she cry in front of him. "I trusted you."

His lips flattened into a thin line. "How did you even find out? It was classified information and there's no way you should have had access to it." Kira had expected an apology, some remorse, an explanation. Not the fury coarsening his voice. Before she could say anything he held up his hand. "Just as I suspected right along. I always wondered why someone with advanced degrees would pretend to be a dog walker. Would barge into my office and agree to become a secretary so readily. I didn't want to believe you had any reason other than your mother's building… If even *that* is the truth."

"I had no—"

The angry downward slash of his arm cut her off. "You pretended you didn't know how to use a phone. You brought in dogs, feigned interest in charities to hide the fact that you were here with an ulterior motive. I knew you weren't interested in me for who I was, but what information you could steal from me."

"Steal? How dare you!"

He narrowed his eyes and shook his head. "No wonder you were so eager to read through every file, to mislead me with your cute little pink sticky notes."

Her fingers trembled and the air caught in her lungs. Was that what he thought of her?

When she didn't respond, he flung more evidence at her. "I lost the strip mall to baseball fields. And the grocery store next to the library? That sweet deal turned sour."

She paused and took a breath. Those had happened before she'd started working for him. She opened her mouth to defend herself but realized that wasn't the point. "Why would you think those were because of me?"

"Because I can do research, too." He stormed over to his desk and opened the top drawer. Then, he tossed the same email with the list of names she'd seen in Tish's office. "Does the name Dominic Layton ring a bell?"

Her heart hung heavy in her chest, and she saw the futility in arguing with him. "My dad?"

"The consulting conglomerate." He spat the words at her.

They'd already addressed her working for Layton Enterprises. "I don't understand—"

"At any time, you could've clued me in to what I was up against." He cut her off and rubbed his forehead.

He meant that she hadn't made idle threats about stopping his company's winning bid to city council. But her dad had signed. There was no reason for him to be upset. She was the one who'd been betrayed.

"I…" She couldn't make sense of everything whirling in her brain. She stepped forward.

He stepped back. "Do you deny you misrepresented who you were?"

She was flabbergasted. He'd not only betrayed her, he'd turned his betrayal into her fabricated crime. She'd trusted him, yet he thought she was, what? Some sort of corporate spy? She held up a hand. "No. You know what? I don't care. I never should've cared. I shouldn't have trusted you. I don't know what I was thinking. I quit."

His eyes narrowed to a slit. "You can't quit because I'm firing you. Pack your things up and go. Now. Before I have you brought up on charges."

When Tish entered the bedroom, Kira tried to act like she had everything under control, but the ache in her heart wouldn't stop. They'd planned to have Friday night pizza with some other girls from the building, but she didn't want to move from her bed. With quiet steps, her friend approached and sank onto the bed.

"What can I do to help?" she asked, lifting Teddy the Tea Cup Yorkie from the pillow. The puppy licked Tish's face and then settled into her arms.

Kira shook her head without lifting it from her arm.

"Nothing."

"Did you really quit?"

"He...he fired me. He thought I was s-stealing information." Why had he turned out to be such an asshat?

Tish's eyes bugged out as Kira told her about Blake's accusations. "That's ridiculous. I'll march into the office and—"

She clenched her teeth. "No. I don't care what he thinks. I trusted him and he betrayed me." It hurt to find out too late what Blake really thought of her. That he could so easily accuse her of stealing information from him because she wanted to thwart his business dealings.

"Keith was super pissed. He wanted Blake to reason with you. He'll be furious to find out how his brother reacted. Everyone knows how honest you are."

"He's the liar." Kira rolled onto her back and stared at the ceiling. "The only reason I took the job was to save the building on my own." She grabbed Teddy and kissed the top of her head. "I grew up there. Ran around The Fresh Bean after school. I can't let it go. It's where—" She sniffled. "It's where my mom died."

"I know." Tish rubbed the dog's belly.

The familiar feeling of emptiness washed over her. Her entire life she'd tried to find where she fit in, how she mattered. She'd thought she'd finally found someone who understood her dichotomy. But she'd been wrong. "Part of me isn't surprised. Why am I not surprised?"

"I don't know. I'm surprised."

Why had she expected him to hold up his end of the deal? Why hadn't she taken preventative measures against the group sale of the street? It hurt that he'd responded to her accusations with his own baseless slurs. She'd wasted so much time. She could have used these past months to rally support for the building. Gathered interested parties to help her preserve the building as a local landmark. At the very least, told her father about her plans.

She shouldn't have taken the easy way out with that job. She shouldn't have been taken in by his gorgeous eyes and easy smile. She hated how much it cheapened what they'd shared to have Blake betray her. She'd really thought they might…what? She rolled off the bed and forced herself to follow Tish into the living room. Just sex. She and Blake had just sex. A quick fling and an angry goodbye. No need for her to make this more than it was.

Except she was pretty sure she hated him.

B lake sat at a table outside The Fresh Bean and stared at his phone. It hadn't taken long before Keith laid into him for what he'd said to Kira, especially after Tish called in tears and confessed to being the one who'd mentioned the confidential board negotiations. He shouldn't have let his temper get the better of him, but after all Kira had done in the past to stymie his acquisitions, it was only natural to think the worst of her.

But he was wrong. She was guileless. She had a good heart. She fostered dogs. Tish confided she'd given up a high-powered career to do volunteer and pro bono work.

Yet, even as Blake acknowledged his accusations were hurtful, he hadn't called her to explain that he was still working with the board to get them behind the new architectural plans. He'd wanted to, but she'd called him a liar. *A liar.* If she thought *he* was guilty of "lying by omission," well, so was she.

After all they'd shared—hell, he'd adopted a dog with a heart condition, opened his pockets wider for all the charities close to her heart, even told her he wanted a closer relationship—she hadn't trusted him enough to ask about his plans for the board meeting. She'd just railed at him, like he hadn't cared enough to help her. Hadn't cared enough to ask.

He'd always been truthful with her, hadn't said anything about the building because he was convinced he'd win the day for her. Kira was the one who'd been less than open about her past.

So many times since she stormed out of his office, he'd wanted to go back in time and change how he'd reacted. But when he went to pick up the phone, he reminded himself that all that mattered to her were the dogs and the building. If he mattered, if she really cared, she wouldn't have been so quick to quit.

So here he was, at her favorite coffee shop, in front of her mother's building, still trying to make up his mind what to do…or say. Because whenever he thought about facing every day without Kira to greet in the morning and hold in his arms at night, he knew he was lost. Maybe she'd walk up, they'd find some way to brush it off through rational negotiation, and she could come back to his office. And his bed.

When she appeared from somewhere—inside?—he tossed his phone face down on the table and stood.

"Kira!" Damn. He'd hoped to deal with her on a pragmatic business level, like they'd managed for months, even after they'd tumbled into his bed. Without emotion. Cool. Calm. But just seeing her thrilled him, and he had a hard time keeping his voice even.

"I just came from the animal shelter. You took Cyclops." Instead of smiling at him, demonstrating her willingness to put their professional grievances aside, she glared at him. She should be beaming that he'd continued to foster dogs despite their argument. That showed he cared about the same things she did, right?

Worse, she hurled more accusations. An excited bark echoed from under the table. Blake smiled, pulled a dog treat from his pocket, and held it in his hand. The Great Dane gave a happy bark and devoured the snack before settling back down.

He shrugged. "Krystal showed up with him this morning, and I couldn't say no. I mean, look at the poor guy. Nowhere to go and Thanksgiving's tomorrow."

A cone prevented Cyclops from scratching at the eye patch, and Blake reached under the table and ran his hand along the dog's back then rubbed the Dane's head. "Good guy, hey. Yeah. No more skunks, right?"

"Why would you take another foster? You still have Honeybear! Have you forgotten she can't be excited? How will it be for her to have another dog around?"

He couldn't believe she cared more about the dogs than about him, after what they'd shared, but if that was the way she wanted to play, then he'd follow suit. He wasn't about to beg her. This just proved he'd been right all along to not mix business with pleasure. If she thought quitting was the solution, then he'd let her go.

"Yes. I adopted Honeybear, and I'm fostering Cyclops."

"Why?"

No. He would not have this conversation like this. With her half ready to throw a tantrum. This just proved she didn't understand him at all. Had no clue how he felt about these animals. How much he cared about her. She was so ready to condemn him. Maybe he didn't know her after all.

Seeing her—feeling all those tumultuous terrible/wonderful emotions that just her nearness evoked—made him wish he'd never bumped into her that first day. His life had been just fine before her. And now…now, he found himself wanting to call her, to pop out of his office just to see her face. He, damn it, dare he say *needed* her? No. He didn't need anything. While he may have cared for her—more so than he'd thought possible—that didn't mean she reciprocated.

"I don't need to explain myself to you." She wanted all business. He was damn good at that.

She huffed and even stomped her little foot. Before he would've considered it cute, but now he only grudgingly admired the way she kept her gaze neutral and didn't back down. This was the Kira who had first entered his office demanding he save The Bromwell Building. Just one more female wanting something from him.

"Fine. Fine! You're right." She stormed back inside The Fresh Bean.

Well, that was interesting. Why had she come out? To yell at him about Cyclops?

He couldn't replace what he felt for Kira with dogs, but it hurt. Her lack of faith and trust in him. Here he'd been thinking they had a chance, that they could deal with their disagreement in a logical manner and she'd brush off their differences and come back to work for him. In the end, really, she'd only ever had her eye on the prize, like all the other women he'd ever gotten involved with.

If he hadn't been looking at his phone, holding Cyclops's leash, and balancing a coffee in the crook of his arm, Blake might have seen Margie before she stepped in front of him. As it was, he barely managed not to spill anything on him or the dog as he adjusted his balance to avoid the potential collision.

"Hello, Blake." His former secretary smiled at him. "I'm surprised to see you out of the office in the middle of the day. What bet did you lose?"

"Bet? What are you talking about?"

"The dog. Sunlight. Two things I never connected with my former workaholic boss, Blake Whitman. You know? The guy who doesn't have a family and doesn't care if anyone else does, either."

Ouch. Her words caught him in the gut. He'd bet she'd been waiting to spew those at him all along. Guilt washed over him. Had he really been such a tyrant? Kira had never complained. "You're right, aren't you? I'm sorry if I was difficult or too demanding."

Surprise lit her features. "Oh, it wasn't entirely your fault. In the beginning, I welcomed the excuse to stay late. It meant my husband made dinner for me and the kids. But not every night. That got old fast. I tried to tell you that you needed balance. To play. To work less and enjoy more. You don't want to end up both old and alone."

He'd really used her time unfairly. "I really am sorry."

Her mouth curved into a smile, but he couldn't tell if it was real and happy, or fake with a hint of sadness. "I'm sure you had no trouble replacing me. And I'm happy now. I work regular hours, I'm home while it's still light outside, and I don't feel like every item on my agenda has to be finished right then and there. My youngest is learning to play the piano, and I've signed up for a yoga class."

Good for her for finding balance in life. At least she knew what she wanted. Everyone had their own priorities, and until Kira, his had been work.

Cyclops tugged on the leash, and Blake stepped back. "Well, it was nice seeing you."

"You, too. And good luck. You'll find someone smart who'll stick around."

"Thanks for that."

On the way back to the office, he found a park bench and sat to consider Margie's parting words. The Dane plopped down and laid his coned head on Blake's lap.

Absently patting the dog's back, he said, "You know, Cyclops, I found the perfect combination. Kira, the gorgeous woman you just met? She's smart and sexy and grabbed my attention the moment she tripped me." The Dane nuzzled his palm. "Okay. So I broke my own rules by getting involved with her, when I knew business and pleasure don't mix. Ever. But there it is. I did. And blurred lines or not…?"

The dog snorted.

"You're right. I. Do. Not. Give. A. Damn."

Cyclops's massive front paws propped on his thigh, so Blake switched to a belly rub.

"Yeah, we were explosive in bed, and even after the great sex, she never pressured me for a commitment. She was perfect at keeping work and play separate. She was perfect."

The Dane whined, and he squinted at the dog.

"You think I was wrong to let her go?"

Cyclops turned his head and regarded him with big brown eyes, as if agreeing he was an idiot.

Margie's words circled in his head. *"You don't want to end up both old and alone."*

He didn't want to end up old. Without Kira. And he certainly didn't want to end up alone.

If they couldn't discuss getting back together in a business-like manner, or through him fostering Cyclops, he'd have to find some other way to get through to Kira that he needed her in his life. Because he loved her.

Chapter Nineteen

B lake checked his watch for the tenth time in ten seconds. Where the hell was Keith? It was almost four, and City Hall closed at five. If Blake wasn't in a great mood from a recent discussion with one of the undecided board members, he'd be annoyed, but he was one phone call closer to getting the vote to land in his favor. No way would he say anything to Kira until he was absolutely sure.

But he needed his brother to sign a document for the historic downtown redevelopment so he could fix things with her, and the sooner Keith showed up, the better.

The enormity of what he planned to do hit him full force. If this worked, he might be ending his lucrative deal with the city. He might be voted out of the CEO position by the board. He could lose everything on something that might not even get her back.

But he wouldn't think about that now.

Kira strolled along the waterfront and watched the people pass her by. She took a deep breath and released it. This strip of land would be remarkable, no matter how it was designed; it was time to figure out her next course of action. She wasn't angry anymore. She even understood why Blake hadn't told her about the board's indecision and responded with anger instead of apologizing when she accused him of lying. That was a business strategy—put someone on the defensive. Sure, he should have dealt with her from his heart, but the lines between them had blurred so much it was hard to tell what role they were supposed to play: boss and secretary or lover and lover.

So while she forgave Blake for his lack of total honesty, she was depressed that he hadn't done anything to try to get her back. No apology, other than showing up at The Fresh Bean with another dog. Obviously he'd decided his life would be less complicated without her in it. And yes, she'd known all along that the reason he didn't mix sex and employees was to keep things complication-free, but he'd already blurred the lines with her, and until they'd messed things up, they'd been doing fine.

Could she get any part of that back?

With the sun setting over the Gulf of Mexico, Kira changed direction toward The Bromwell Building. Just thinking about the place brought back images of Blake and the scene of the crime. The first place she'd plowed into him. The last place she'd seen him with Cyclops, and many times in between.

If she applied for landmark status, the building would be protected, and Blake couldn't do one damn thing to tear it down. But her dad had already agreed to the group sale, and she doubted he'd be willing to take this to court. Plus, even if she won, she'd be stabbing Blake in the back with his board. Forcing his hand to construct around the building rather than based on his company's recommendations.

She couldn't do that to him. Not when she'd rather tear off her own arm than see him fail.

How had she let him become so important to her? Her throat tightened. Caring about him so much left her with few options.

As she approached the building, tears blurred her vision. The cute cafe tables. The brick storefront. Even from the sidewalk, she could smell the coffee.

A figure stepped into her path, and she looked up to meet Blake's guarded eyes, a stony expression on his face. Her feet stopped moving, and she choked back her surprise.

He stared at her for a long moment and then said, "I couldn't let you walk by without saying hi."

Her heart tore open at the way he regarded her, so hesitant. She searched his face for something that might reveal his mood. She glanced down at the Great Dane and then squinted up at him. "Um…hi?"

He pressed a hand to his heart. "I'm Blake and this is my rescue dog, Cyclops. I adopted a Chinese Shar Pei, but she's at home because she has a heart condition."

Cyclops sniffed her shoes and then walked around them, the leash effectively locking her in place. She stepped out of the loop, mentally begging Blake to take her in his arms. When he didn't, she said, "Hi, Blake. I'm Kira. Why would you adopt a dog with a heart condition? What if she dies?"

He gazed at her like they'd never argued in the first place, and little bits of hope flowed through her. She couldn't quite believe it when he stepped into her space and touched the side of her face. "She will. But when you love someone, you have to be willing to take the pain that comes with it."

Her heart leaped into her throat. *Love*? Could she hope he was trying to tell her something?

He stepped back and handed her a packet. "I think we should look through this together."

A million thoughts flooding her brain, she sank into one of the cafe chairs and pulled out the top sheet, reading the title, *Authenticating Local Landmarks*. The application had already been filled out and notarized. The filing fee had been stamped as paid.

The Bromwell Building. Date of construction. Significance of use. Nomination guide.

Her eyes blurred as she looked up at Blake and then back to the second page. *Petition for Support*.

The signatures included names she recognized from the historical society, elected officials, and the mayor. Keith's name appeared on a letter to the city council stating how he fully supported Blake's change in architectural design, and as the CFO, he confirmed the cost-benefit analysis for towns with historically designated areas.

But the name that stuck out the brightest was the name of the applicant: Blake Whitman.

She processed the information at a snail's pace, reading and re-reading, digesting it all and finally understanding that Blake had applied to save her building, just as she'd threatened she would do when she confronted him.

Just to be clear, she said, "If this goes through, and your company board votes against the design, you'll lose the bid. The building will be protected, and you won't be able to implement your shiny, new plans."

Blake nodded. "I know, but I don't care. I love you. Being with you means more to me than any building, any position, any job."

She sucked in huge amounts of air, unsure she could fully trust what his actions meant. He'd gone and done exactly what she'd just decided she'd never do. He'd taken steps to protect her building, even if that meant it went against his company's board. In the meantime, they had to wait and in the end, all decisions were out of their hands. The most important thing, though, was that he'd done it because he loved her. He loved her.

She was afraid to breath. Afraid she'd wake up and find out that none of this was real.

He scooted his chair closer to hers, and before she could blink, his mouth covered hers, and his arms tugged her into his chest. She sank into him, eager to get closer. She lost all sense of time and space and only knew that right there, in his embrace, with his lips on hers, she could handle anything. Even the prick of paws on her thigh and the sharp cut of the plastic cone from Cyclops's sloppy attempt to join in the kiss.

They parted slowly, hesitantly, and she laughed at how easy it was for him to make her forget the entire world. The sidewalk, the dog, the building.

He touched his forehead to hers and whispered again, "I love you, and I'm sorry I was an ass."

She blinked back happy tears. "I… I love you, too, and I'm also sorry you were an ass."

His shoulders shook with laughter, and he gave her another kiss before admitting, "You keep me real, Kira. You give me balance, and that's something I've never thought I needed until you."

She swallowed back her choked up emotions. "I should've told you about those other deals, but I never did anything against you when I worked there."

He wrapped an arm around her shoulder and pulled her to him. Staring into her eyes, she saw the sincerity in his words. "I know. I know you. I trust you."

Tears stung her eyes again, and she looked up at the building and then back to his face. "All I wanted to do was be part of something beautiful. I didn't want to let down my mom. I didn't want to let go."

He brushed a strand of hair off her cheek. "You are beautiful, and you don't have to give up anything. I'm going to do everything in my power to make sure you have whatever you want."

She looked back down at the table, at the papers that hadn't disappeared with invisible ink. "I still can't believe—"

He nibbled on the side of her neck. "The downtown district is going to be amazing."

Cyclops made a circle and plopped back on the pavement, halfway landing on her foot.

She cleared her throat. "Because of you. All because of you."

It was almost too much to take in all at once. She wasn't sure she could be any happier than when she was to be in his arms. "But-but what happens now?"

He grinned and stood. "Now? We go back to my place, and I'll cook you dinner." He held out his free hand, and she reached to clasp it. His skin felt warm as he curled his fingers around hers.

She giggled. "I like to eat. In fact, I'm thinking we should start with dessert first."

"My thoughts exactly. I have a fresh package of coconut macaroons."

"And whipped cream?"

"I'm sure that can be arranged." That sexy smile of his—the one that set her on fire—curved his mouth.

The silly buzz that hummed through her body didn't stop as they continued down the sidewalk side by side. It had always been like this between them, and every time she thought she'd gotten her desire under control, something would happen to let her know the chemistry hadn't waned.

It probably never would.

Epilogue

Edgewater Bay's Downtown District
One year later

The sun cast bright light over the early morning volunteers setting up for the Bayfront Festival and Ribbon Cutting. Most of the buildings had been renovated to meet the current Florida Building Code without losing their original structure or facade, and this morning marked the first day for Bayfront Boulevard to be reopened to the public.

Blake stood with his back to the sun, his eyes pinned on the one woman capable of distracting him from anything and everything. She moved with liquid grace, unrolling the thick, red ribbon for the mayor to cut in a couple of hours. If it weren't for her, so many things would be different, including his apartment with three dogs, but she'd wiggled her way into his life, and he couldn't imagine spending his time any other way than with her.

When she moved to haul a crate, he jumped into action, stopping her before she could bend in a bad way.

Jogging over to her, he called, "Let me get that."

She whirled on him and grinned. "I got it. You just relax and prepare for your speech."

His speech. How could he think about a speech when he'd noticed that pink stick in the trash bin? He could hardly believe that after a year together they were adding to their family, and not just with more dogs. They'd had a serious conversation when a board position for the animal rescue opened, because within the first week, Kira had filled his apartment with a dozen dogs, violating the city ordinance.

"I've got it right here." He tapped his back pocket with the rolled up pages of his speech.

Suspicion filled her voice as she asked, "Have you reviewed all my notes?"

"A good deal of them." Truthfully, he hadn't looked at the thing in two days. They'd been too busy, and with one thing after another, he hadn't made the dedication speech a priority.

Her mouth curved into an adorable pout, and she wrapped her arms around his waist. "I think you should review it one more time." She used the hug to snatch the paper from his pocket and presented it to him. "Over here."

Steering him by the shoulders, she pushed him in the direction she wanted him to go.

He spun around and faced her, holding the speech but not looking at it. "Ladies and gentlemen, I am honored to present to you—"

He glanced down and saw her trademark pink flower sticky note, which she'd used to mark his stage direction. He knew them by heart. The first one read, "Scan the crowd with your eyes, so they know you're looking at all of them." But as the speech came to an end, he saw she'd replaced the final sticky with a different note. Next to the words, "…for our families to enjoy for generations," she'd placed a baby blue rattle-shaped sticky note that read, "including my son, due this summer."

The pages fell from his fingers and he wrapped her in the full-body hug. "I love you so much."

"Thank you for making all my dreams come true."

"*Our* dreams, Kira. Ours."

Acknowledgments

First and forever, thank you to all the readers and writers and believers in the power of words.

Nicole and Robin, you stuck with this to the end, and I am grateful for your immeasurable talents that shaped this book. Without your guidance, I wouldn't have made it to today. Thank you.

Always, to Simon Cleveland, my first reader and my last everything.

About the Author

Marisa Cleveland loves to laugh, hates to cry, and does both often. She's been called admissions counselor, assistant director, teacher, coach, analyst, agent, friend, and wife. As a writer, she writes. Every day.

Perhaps because she married her best friend, her adult romance novels focus on playfully naughty relationships developed through friendship and family-oriented values. She is a member of SCBWI, RWA, and YARWA.

www.marisacleveland.com